To Chloe
Thank you ____nt
tell you how much your
support means to me ♡

Love in the Wings

Ellie White

Lave ♂
Ellie /b

Ellie White

Love in the Wings

Copyright © 2023 Elizabeth White

All rights reserved.

ISBN: 9798376712221

Imprint: E White Publishing

Editing: Aimee Walker

Cover Design: Yummy Book Covers

For Oliver and Hallie, this is a reminder that you can do anything you set your mind to.

Dear Reader,

Over the past year I have spent countless hours researching the world of musical theatre to make this story realistic and a special thanks goes out to Katie Brace from Katie Brace Creatives and Steph Durkin from the Sunderland Empire.

Saying that, this is a work of fiction and some scenarios have been exaggerated for added drama and tension (sexy mic fitting? Yes please, but probably not in real life.)

This story also includes scenes of parental abandonment, emotional abuse and control at the hands of a parent, cancer and subsequent death of a parent, swearing and an open-door sex scene, if this is a trigger for you, please make an informed choice before reading.

I hope you love this book and these characters as much as I have enjoyed creating them!

Love,
Ellie

Ellie White

CHAPTER ONE
Liam

I knew this would happen again and yet the news still manages to knock the wind right out of my sails.

It's the reason I'm out running at eight on a Monday morning, knowing fine well I've got a twelve-to-fourteen-hour day ahead of me. Punishing myself by tearing my lungs apart from the inside for being such a bloody idiot. I don't know why I expected this production to be any different to the last or the ones before that.

Am I such a fool for believing him? For believing Dad when he said I would be deputy stage manager on this tour. Yeah, I am, because I expected him to keep his word even though I know better than anyone that his word is useless. I should have gotten it in writing.

He couldn't even call me himself to let me down gently, he got Di, our stage manager, to email me at midnight last night.

Well fuck that and fuck him.

I take out my frustration by stomping my feet down harder with every step I take on the cobbled pier, never taking my eye off my destination, a red and white stone lighthouse that stands proud at the end.

That's it, I'm totally done. When I've finished this run, I'm going to go back there and quit.

Fuck Dad, fuck the production.

I'm. Done.

I use my rage to push through the pain in my protesting thighs and calves and continue running towards Roker lighthouse and the horizon behind it. I've been running in this heat for half an hour now and I'm struggling to breathe – each intake of air is like inhaling fire, but I don't stop, I need to feel this.

I come to an abrupt stop when I round the right side of the lighthouse, keeping my eyes locked on the water. I grip onto the black wrought-iron railing, my chest heaving. Then I let it all out.

I scream at the black water stretching out for miles in front of me. Even the sea is mocking me with its calmness.

Giving in to the breathless feeling, my lungs continue to burn as they strain to take in oxygen. "Fuck! Fuck! Fuck!"

I run a hand through my longer than normal hair, now saturated with sweat much like the rest of my body. I collapse to the floor against the slabs of white granite that make up the foot of Roker lighthouse and close my eyes. Taking in a few deep breaths, I stretch my legs and let them out slowly, remembering the cool down breathing exercises they taught us in my childhood drama school.

The longer I keep my eyes closed, the more details my other senses pick up, things I hadn't noticed when I let my rage blind me. The smell of salty seaside air and seaweed waft around me. I almost melt into the granite against my back as I listen to the relaxing sounds of the waves lapping against the rocks at the base of the pier. Before I know it, my breathing has matched the rhythm of the waves and I'm a lot calmer. The sun, already high above the horizon, beats down and warms my skin and every so often the sea spray mists my face as though it knows I need to cool off.

I don't know how long I sit in the same spot, but a quick glance at my watch tells me I'm going to be late. Heaving myself up again, my legs try to protest as I jog back along the pier to Roker Terrace in the direction of the theatre.

Not that it matters that I'm going to be late, I'm quitting, right?

I've worked as an assistant stage manager for Whitton Productions for twelve years, since I was eighteen. At first it was an unpaid internship while I studied stage management at uni, then after I graduated, I was made a permanent crew member. I'm now thirty and by this point of my career, I wanted to have worked my way up to stage manager, but my dad, Mr Whitton himself, still doesn't think I'm ready for more responsibility.

After twelve long years, I know I'm ready and I know I'm great at my job, but Dad has never believed in me, even when I was a kid he always put me down.

That's how I knew this would happen, because it's been happening for years.

At the beginning of a production, Dad would promise I'd get a promotion on the next show if I did a decent job. I'd always go above and beyond, yet it was never enough because by the time we'd move on to the next show, suddenly, I'm not getting that promotion and Di, our stage manager and dad's closest friend, has to be the one to tell me. Whenever I ask why he can't tell me himself, the answer is that Dad has enough on his plate managing the production company and the chain of Whitton Theatres dotted around the country, that he can't get involved with "staffing matters".

"Staff!" I'm his son for crying out loud.

And that… is why I'm definitely quitting today!

CHAPTER TWO
Harriet

I gasp excitedly as "What Dreams Are Made Of" from *The Lizzie McGuire Movie* blasts unexpectedly through the car speakers. My younger sister Jayne, who is sitting in the back seat, looks nonchalantly out the window, her face eventually cracking into a coy smile.

"Oh, come on this is perfect," I squeal excitedly as I jump out of the car and throw open her door, tugging her by the hand to dance in the deserted coastal car park. She's trying her best not to enjoy herself but not fooling anyone; she is loving this as much as I am.

By the time the second verse kicks in she's committed and the two of us flail our arms around in the air singing as loud as our voices can go. Neither of us care that a few passing dog walkers stop to gawk at us as we frolic.

"If you tell anyone that I was singing along to Lizzie McGuire and that I knew the words, I swear to god, Harriet, I will end you," Jayne says once the song has finished and we're back in the car. She leans between the front seats to threaten me, and I sarcastically mime the words back to her.

"Less of the threats of violence, Jayne," Mam scolds,

11

laughing nonetheless. It's been a few months since I returned home from London with my tail between my legs. I think it's a relief for Mam to have me back in my childhood bedroom after what I went through down there.

Jayne and I were born less than a year apart and have always been super close despite not sharing one common interest. The only thing we did have in common growing up was our looks, and due to the short age gap, we were often mistaken for twins. Thanks to Dad, we have matching blue-green eyes and both sit around the five foot seven mark, although our olive complexion and thick dark hair comes from Mam.

The twin thing ended in our early twenties when I kept my mid-length, naturally wavy hair and Jayne chose to chop hers into a shoulder-length bob and lighten it with coppery highlights.

Jayne's phone rings, cutting off the Disney Channel Original Film Soundtrack playlist that had continued to play at a low volume in the background.

"Dad's video calling me," Jayne says, leaning through the gap between the front seats again and stretching her arm forward to get me in the shot with her.

"Hi, Dad," we both chorus like we're auditioning for *Charlie's Angels*. "I thought you'd be still sleeping," I add.

"I wouldn't miss this for the world," he says, sounding tired and hoarse. "Are you there now?"

Jayne taps the screen, swapping the camera to face out the windscreen, focusing on Whitton Theatre standing proudly on the cliff in front of us. Even in the tiny phone screen, I can see his face light up with pride.

"I'm so proud of you, Harriet. I'm sorry I couldn't come with you," he says, sadness taking over his shallow features. He fights back a yawn followed by a pained grimace he quickly disguises. I look at Mam concerned, but she shakes her head, telling me not to say anything. His pain has worsened lately, and he's trying his best to mask it.

"When I get my bearings, I'll video call and give you a tour backstage," I say, and he smiles. "Okay, tell your mother not to rush home, I'm going to go back to sleep now. I love you, and break a leg."

"Love you too, Dad."

Swallowing the lump that has formed in my throat, I blow a kiss to the screen and he returns it before shutting off the call.

Dad has always loved this place, we would come to Whitton Theatre together to watch all kinds of shows, sometimes it was just me and Dad, other times Mum and Jayne would come too. There were even times when Dad and I would be driving past for a completely unrelated reason and pull over into the car park just to look at it.

It's a tall, grand-looking building with four Graeco-Roman pillars. In summer, each column is decorated with a rainbow array of flowers spiralling around the sand-coloured stone. In winter the flowers are replaced by a Christmas garland and fairy lights ready for panto season.

Although I'm no stranger to this theatre, today is my first time here as a performer, which is why it's so important for Dad too.

"Thank you for coming with me this morning," I say to Mam and Jayne, unable to put into words how much it means that they're here sharing this moment with me. The lump in my throat only tightens when I look at them.

"I wouldn't miss this for the world, Harriet," Mam says, tears filling her eyes.

I know she's thinking about Dad when she looks out of the windshield with a heavy sigh.

"Okay, I'm ready to go in," I say, taking a deep, grounding breath and straightening my spine. I get out of the car and close the door behind me, as do Jayne and Mam.

"I want photos," Jayne says with a shrug, waving her camera around when I look at her quizzically. "This low morning sun is amazing, and I'm really proud of you, so I'd like a photograph please."

She doesn't wait for my response, instead she links my arm with a wide grin and steers me in the right direction. When I'm standing at the top of the steps by the grand entrance, Jayne has me pose in a variety of positions as she snaps away, calling out commands and encouragement that proves she does this for a living.

"I'm not going to mess it up this time, Mam, I promise," I say once the impromptu photoshoot is finished. I don't know who I'm trying to convince more, me or her.

"*You* didn't mess it up last time either," she says, but it still doesn't change what happened in London. "Sometimes we make a mistake and trust the wrong people. It's okay to feel nervous, you've been through the wringer, but learn from your mistakes, don't dwell on them. Now get in there and have a wonderful first day, sweetheart."

Learn from my mistakes... so don't fall in love with any more theatre guys then. Easy.

"I love you."

"Love you too," she says, kissing my cheek and giving me one last maternal squeeze. "Break a leg!"

"I'll pick you up later, same spot," Jayne calls after me and I wave to them both as I walk down the narrow side street towards the back of the theatre. I don't go straight in, instead I cross the cobbled road to the path opposite the stage door, so I can take a picture for Dad.

It's exactly how I remember it! Mam and Dad would always wait with me after a show and take my picture when the stars would come out. I remember thinking it was so cool to meet these larger-than-life people who got to perform for a living. I wanted to be like them so badly.

I kept all my pictures in a scrapbook – my favourite is a picture of me and my little sister when we met Ant and Dec after a pantomime. I was about ten or eleven at the time, and Jayne insisted on wearing her Sunderland AFC football kit, knowing that Ant and Dec are probably the most famous Newcastle United fans around. She's standing there with her hands on her hips sticking her tongue out at the famous duo who are pretending to cry. I laughed so hard in that moment that I almost wet myself.

Maybe one day, some little girl will wait out here for a photograph with me. I can only hope I inspire them as much as I've been inspired by others in my life.

I snap a quick selfie with the blue light box that reads "Stage Door" visible in the background, my grin so wide it reaches my eyes. I lean back in the shadows against the cooling stone of the building and send it to Dad before posting it on my Instagram page too, making a silent promise to myself that this time, I'm not going to mess it up.

And then, because I'm a theatre kid, I take in another dramatic deep breath and step forward, the first step towards my dream, which a few months ago I was so sure I'd never see again.

CHAPTER THREE
Harriet

"Umph!" A deep voice exclaims as I'm unexpectedly knocked off my feet the second I step out of the shadows. My arms flail and a pathetic little squeal escapes my throat as the stranger and I attempt to stay upright to no avail. We grasp for each other as we try to save ourselves but it's too late.

After what feels like an eternity of tumbling in slow motion, I land on my backside on the pavement, with a gorgeous man lying on top of me. Momentarily dumbstruck, the first thing I notice about this bearded man with dark-brown mussed-up hair, is that he has the most beautifully deep and expressive eyes, even if right now they are panic stricken. They're hazel with gold specks and although I should be alarmed there is a random man lying on top of me in the street, as I gaze into them, I'm surprisingly calm.

Probably because both of us are frozen in shock for an agonisingly long time in this extremely intimate position, where he is nestled between my thighs and I've all but crossed my ankles behind his back to keep him there. One of his large hands is cradling my head preventing my skull from shattering against the concrete beneath me, his other hand is planted on the pavement above my shoulder, holding his weight above me so I'm not squashed beneath him. Literally every nerve ending in my body is tingling.

"I'm-so-sorry," he says quickly as if it's all one word. When he realises the position we've landed in, he leaps up awkwardly, putting some much-needed space between us.

As an afterthought, he extends his hand towards me to help me up.

Now that he isn't an inch from my face, I'm suddenly aware that I'm lying on the ground looking all desperate and bereft like a damsel in distress. Embarrassment engulfs me and for some reason unknown to me, that embarrassment turns to defensiveness.

"You need to watch where you're going when you're running out of alleyways!" I snap, ignoring the gorgeous stranger's outstretched hand.

"Maybe you should be the one to watch where you're going, after all, you did step right into me as I ran down the street." Amusement coats his words; he's even smirking at me, which only makes my cheeks burn hotter.

Avoiding his gaze, I pick myself up and dust off my bum before bending down to pick up the bundle of dance shoes tied together with their laces that fell from my shoulder in the fall.

"Are you okay?" he asks, sounding concerned now as I avoid eye contact with him completely. I huff and puff a little more, struggling to get my shoes to stay put instead of slipping from my shoulder repeatedly.

Risking a glance at him from behind the mop of curly hair that's fallen over my shoulder, I notice he looks concerned too.

My body feels like it's about to set on fire, so I slip off the cardigan I stupidly wore in a heatwave and tie it around my hips. Christ, this is mortifying, and I need to get out of here.

"Yes, I'm fine. Please excuse me. I have somewhere to be."

This is going to be okay, I tell myself. Keep avoiding all eye contact, walk away and obsess over this moment right before I fall asleep every night for the rest of my life. That seems like a healthy response.

I hang my dance shoes around my neck by their laces where they finally stay put and straighten my duffel bag. Then I dart past the man and cross over the road as quickly as my feet will carry me, ignoring the pain niggling in my right hip.

Perfect, just what I need on the first day of tech week.

I hear him let out a low chuckle as he follows closely behind me.

"Excuse me. Are you following me?" I ask, stopping abruptly and turning to face him when I reach the two small steps to the stage door. He's definitely following me, there is nowhere else for him to be going.

He screeches to a halt and stumbles forward slightly, grabbing a hold of my shoulders so he doesn't knock me over again. Luckily, even though both of us sway on the spot, we remain upright this time.

My breath catches in my throat and my heart speeds up, I'm not sure if it's from the sudden close contact or shock, either way my body should not be reacting like this at all to a strange man in the street. Where are my danger senses? Surely a man following me should ring some alarm bells, but instead I can't stop thinking about how his firm hands feel as he holds me and how hard his body felt lying on top of me only a moment ago.

He's close enough that I can smell the musky scent of his skin again and I have a sudden urge to swipe my index finger down his bare arm, to trace the lines of his muscles and tendons below his soft tanned skin.

Jesus Christ! Get it together, woman.

Composing my thoughts, I plant my hands firmly on my hips and narrow my eyes at him, trying my best to look intimidating, but the way his lip quirks up in amusement tells me I'm not as intimidating as I think I am.

"We're actually heading to the same place." He nods to the door behind me.

Oh, for fuck's sake, this is fantastic.

I embarrass myself in front of him, then I internally accuse him of being a stalker and all along he works here.

"Oh, right, well… I'll continue walking then," I say, the intense heat of the blush in my cheeks again.

"Why don't we walk together? Then I won't have to worry about crashing into you for a third time."

I consider his proposition for a second. "Right… Okay then… that would be agreeable."

Oh, good god, *that would be agreeable*, now I really do want the ground to swallow me whole. This man has turned my brain to mush.

"I started to say that would be fine and then changed to I agree mid-sentence," I explain.

My gaze drops to the tops of my arms that he's still holding, and he quickly pulls his hands back from my shoulders.

I turn to the door but stop and glance over my shoulder at him. If I weren't already crushing hard on this man, the sight in front of me now would be enough to do it. He's not watching me, so I let my eyes roam all over him and enjoy the show. He lifts the hem of his dark-grey tank top to wipe the sweat from his brow, and holy hell… This man is something else! His biceps flex and his stomach is tight and firm without being overly muscular, the kind of body you get from manual labour, not spending hours in a gym.

Time moves in slow motion and I swear I can hear Etta James' "I Just Want to Make Love to You" playing in the background like it's a Diet Coke advert and he's the hunky star. All he needs is a silver can, wet with condensation, that he swipes along his brow, before taking a long, deep gulp—

"Shall we?" he asks, breaking me from my trance with an overconfident grin having caught me brazenly checking him out. My jaw is slack and my feet are rooted to the spot. I seem to have lost my voice, but I can nod. He leans past me reaching for the handle – his forearm grazes the skin on my waist not covered by my cropped t-shirt – and pulls open the door. Placing his back against the open door to hold it open, he motions for me to enter. It's an old building so the doors are narrow, I have no choice but to slide through facing him.

Do I *accidentally* brush my boobs against him? Obviously.

It takes a great amount of effort to turn away from him once I'm through the door without doing something stupid like licking his bicep or inhaling his neck, the scent of his woody aftershave mixed with fresh workout sweat is almost too much to bear at such a close distance.

I bet he tastes as delicious as he smells.

I'm snapped from my perverted daydreams when I hear a throat clearing, both of us turn our heads to look at a young girl leaning out of a small window that connects this entryway to the stage door keeper's office. She waves seductively at my new friend, and he gives her a friendly smile back before turning to me and introducing her as Stage Door Steph.

"I'm Harriet, Harriet Adams," I say with a polite smile before I lean down and tick off my details on the sign-in sheet that's already waiting for me.

The phone on her desk rings and she shoots an apologetic look before answering, which I don't think is for my benefit.

Leaving Steph behind us, we walk down the warren of corridors that form backstage. He navigates us expertly, despite all the walls being the same clean and clinical shades of white with blue linoleum floors.

"So, you're the Harriet Adams I've heard so much about then?" He breaks the silence.

I can feel the colour immediately drain from my face at his choice of words. What could he know? The whole London debacle was supposed to be kept quiet by my previous production company, no one else was supposed to find out about my fall from grace besides those of us in the room when it happened. I kept to my side of the bargain and kept my mouth shut so I wouldn't embarrass the company, they were supposed to keep theirs too.

"What?" I ask. The walls are shrinking around me and the air thinning.

Another concerned look appears on his face. "Shit, not in a bad way, obviously. Katie is my cousin," he elaborates quickly, reassuring me. Katie is my fellow swing in the show, and we've become close friends in the three weeks of rehearsals we've recently completed.

Relief floods me to know that my secret is still that, a secret.

"Oh, right. You're Liam then?" My heart gradually returns to its normal rhythm. "She mentioned you."

"Yeah. I'm ASM in the show." I can tell he's trying to not draw attention to my reaction, but I've definitely ruined the vibe between us.

"You didn't come to the rehearsal studio."

"I was busy here. My…" he pauses, "I help with theatre maintenance every now and then. I worked on the renovation a few years back, so I get called in when things need fixing on the odd occasion."

"Wow, that's amazing you got to be a part of that."

"Yeah, it really was. I was between productions at the time, so it was my way of staying in the theatre without the shows. I got to see the place stripped right back to its bones. We uncovered a lot of original features and even some portraits of famous thespians that had been painted over by someone in the seventies. We knew they were there from pictures of opening night but seeing them being gradually uncovered was amazing."

On our walk through the theatre, we make a quick diversion to the green room so Liam can show me where I can hang out when I'm not on stage or don't have a scheduled performance. The walls are decorated with old show posters signed by their cast and has a bookshelf full to the brim with house programmes that I can't wait to dive into. For entertainment there is a pool table and a large TV in front of a large comfortable-looking couch, as well as a few bistro-style tables and chairs for eating meals. There's even a little kitchen with a fridge, microwave and kettle. It's everything you want in a home away from home, because reality is, we'll be spending more time with our fellow cast and crew here than our families at home.

As we continue, Liam is a perfect gentleman, pointing out small but interesting things in the room and giving me a little history lesson as we go, little facts I never learned from the tours I took, and I make mental notes to tell my dad when I get home.

I'm completely captivated by Liam, the way speaks so passionately about this place, the dimple he gets in his cheek when he smiles and the little scar above his left eyebrow that I have an unrelenting urge to brush my thumb over. I imagine every girl he meets feels just like I do, like a teenage girl with her first crush.

Five minutes later, much to my disappointment, we reach a dressing room and Liam taps the laminated sign taped to it that has my name on it. I'm not ready for this to be over.

"Here we are," he says, before he's cut off by a voice in the distance calling his name.

"You're late, Liam."

Diane, our stage manager, stands at the end of the corridor, one hand on her hip as she looks between us with an eyebrow raised in curiosity. "I see you've finally met our wonderful assistant stage manager?" she adds to me. I don't know why but with her looking right at me, I feel like a kid caught with their hand in the biscuit tin.

"Yeah, Liam was kind enough to show me to my dressing room," I say, feeling the need to explain.

She eyes Liam suspiciously. "When you're done, Liam, I need a word."

"That's me summoned." He gives me another cheeky grin. "I'll be right there, Di," he adds loud enough for her to hear. She remains standing within earshot but is now engrossed in the conversation she's having through her headset.

"Thank you for showing me around."

"It was nice crashing into you, Harriet."

He backs away from me slowly with yet another flirtatious smile gorgeous enough to empty my brain of any coherent thoughts.

CHAPTER FOUR
Liam

Diane stares at me as I come to face her. She is dressed head to toe in typical stage manager black attire, with her headset fixed in place over her sleek blonde bob and an additional handheld radio clipped to her belt. Not to mention the mobile phone, clipboard and iPad held against her body, and her other hand planted firmly on her hip in disapproval.

"What was all that about?" she asks, as we walk side by side towards the door leading to the stairs at the far end of the corridor. The theatre is an old building, but the block containing the dressing rooms is relatively new with floor-to-ceiling glass walls giving the stairway the feel of a greenhouse in the summer.

"What was what about?" I feign innocence.

Obviously, I know exactly what she's talking about, the chemistry between Harriet and me was palpable. I purposely take the stairs ahead of Di two at a time, avoiding her curious gaze.

"I wasn't born yesterday, Liam." She jogs up the remaining stairs to catch up to me.

"We ran into each other on the street, and I walked with her to her dressing room like the gent I am," I explain, and she scoffs.

"So, what was with the 'it was nice crashing into you,

Harriet?'" she asks in a comically deep voice that sounds nothing like me. I roll my eyes. "Look, Liam. I've got your back, I'm constantly fighting for you, but you need to help me out here! If you want him to take you seriously you can't be waltzing in here late because you're too busy flirting with our actresses."

The anger I felt earlier, boils back up again. Let it be known that, although, yes, I was definitely flirting with Harriet, this is the first occasion I've ever flirted with any cast member since I've worked for the company. Not to mention, I've never been late to work.

Ever!

I'm usually half an hour early and I never get so much as a thanks for it.

"I really don't know if you do have my back when it comes to my dad," I say, immediately regretting it when I see the hurt in her eyes. It's not her fault he makes her deliver unwelcome news and, truth be told, I'd rather it come from her than anyone else. But fuck it, I'm mad at her and I'm mad at him and I need to remember that. "I don't know if I can do this anymore, Di, you know I've been offered promotions elsewhere. Promotions I've been an idiot to turn down in the past, but I stay here for him and I'm failing to remember why."

"Are you thinking about quitting?" She seems genuinely surprised. "You'd leave the company founded by and named after your family?"

Now she's outright asked me about quitting, I really don't know what to do anymore. Up until ten minutes ago I was ready to come in here, hand in my notice and get out, but now, walking these familiar corridors with her to the dressing room I've had for years, I don't know if I can do it.

"This theatre and the production company may be named after my ancestors, but I don't share that family name, Di."

My entire life I've been known as Liam Wright, taking Mam's surname instead of Dad's.

"Once this tour is done, he'll promote you, I'll make sure of it. You need to stay out of trouble and work your arse off in the meantime," she promises, but like everything else she says, it's an empty promise.

"I've worked my arse off my entire adult life for him, it's never been enough!" I take out my frustration on my dressing room door, using more force than necessary and slamming it against the wall with a clatter.

"This time will be different, I promise." Another empty promise.

"He says that every tour and here I am, still ASM, and there you are, believing the bullshit that comes out of his mouth." I throw my arms out as I dump my backpack in my locker. She doesn't respond as I continue to throw my strop. "Anyway, I don't know how any of this relates to me speaking to Harriet. She's nice, that's all, okay? I was trying to make her feel welcome, like I would anyone else."

"Fine, but don't get too close to her. There's a reason she's no longer a principal cast member in one of the biggest shows to hit the West End this decade. That's all I can say, so I need you to trust that it's best for you to stay away from her."

If there's one way to make me want something, it's to tell me I can't have it. Now my curiosity over the beautiful brunette with the blue-green eyes is piqued and I want to know more, but not from Di, I want to get to know Harriet directly.

Di takes my silence as her cue to continue.

"Look, I know you're disappointed, but your dad doesn't want people to think you got promoted because you're his son. He wants you to earn it and you can't earn it by getting involved with that girl."

I stare at her in sheer disbelief, taking a few seconds to gather my thoughts so I can keep a sliver of composure.

"I have earned it. I'm good at my job and the fact you're telling me I need to earn it just shows how undervalued I am. Do you expect me to believe Dad is attempting to avoid claims of nepotism by working me harder than any other ASM in the industry? Come on, he's done this my whole life, he dangles enough of a carrot to keep my interest but never lets me catch the reward. Not only that, but no one knows who my dad actually is!" I sigh audibly as I grab a clean set of clothes and towel from my bag. "This is the last time I'm doing this. I'll stay for this run, then I'm done, I'd rather walk away empty handed than be humiliated by my own father... again. And as for telling me who I can and can't talk to, well, you have no grounds to do that," I add, surprisingly calm on the surface but inside I'm a raging inferno.

I guess I've made my decision then. Three months and then I'm done here. For good.

Di stands aside to let me pass through the doorway and I stalk off in the direction of the showers so I can wash away my morning run. She doesn't try to catch up, so I figure she's done talking too.

CHAPTER FIVE
Harriet

This is it, I think, closing the door behind me and taking in the dressing room I'll be sharing with Katie.

I waste no time at all before settling in and unpacking. I have all the essentials: make-up, what looks like a lifetime supply of throat sweets and my Dr Nelson's steamer. I pluck the picture of me, Jayne and our parents out of my purse and tuck it into the edge of the mirror, flicking on the bulbs that border it.

The dressing room is barely big enough for two, but it feels so glamorous. It looks like a set right out of *Moulin Rouge*, I half expect Ewan McGregor (or even better Aaron Tviet) to start serenading me at any given moment.

In front of our mirror, we have a long dressing table that stretches the length of the wall and a chair each, red velvet upholstered, with a matching chaise longue in the corner.

The view from our window looks out to the north, but if you press yourself up against the glass and look east towards the coast there is a tiny sliver of the deep blue sea and golden sand where the Roker and Seaburn beaches meet.

While I wait for Katie to arrive, I smile lovingly at my family photograph. This photo has been with me for every production I've been part of. It keeps me grounded, reminding me why I do this and whose opinion really matters.

Katie strides in a few minutes later, looking way cooler than I could ever dream of. Beats wireless headphones in front of a huge blonde messy bun, singing along to an old Paramore song as she blows a bubble with her chewing gum.

"Sup," she says, tipping her head back with a smile. It's hard not to be happy when faced with her infectious grin and adorable dimples.

"Do people even say 'sup' anymore?"

"I'm bringing it back," she says with a determined nod of the head.

"Are you bringing back your inner emo kid too?" I refer to her hoodie that says 'retired emo kid' with a hand doing the devil horn sign.

"I don't think I ever stopped to be fair, although the dyed black hair was not a good look on a natural blonde with ginger skin." I laugh as she drops her bag haphazardly and plops down onto the chaise lounge, crossing her legs beneath her.

Like me, Katie is a swing and new to the company. It was nice to have a friend in the same position as me this past month in rehearsal since a lot of the other cast members have worked together previously.

We bonded right away over our love of Lin Manuel Miranda, movie musicals and Andrew Garfield. To be more specific... our love of Andrew Garfield in *Tick, Tick, Boom*, a movie musical directed by Lin Manuel Miranda.

Katie groans when a second later there is a call over the speaker announcing that it's time to head to the auditorium. She whips off her emo hoodie to reveal her black skirted ballet leotard and pink tights matching my own. She grabs her hairbrush and expertly neatens her hair into a ballerina bun with a hair doughnut in less than thirty seconds.

It's so typically Katie. In the brief time I've known her, I've seen this transition from bubbly, talks a million miles a minute, self-confessed weirdo who doesn't give two fucks about anything, into a prima ballerina that looks a lot like Tinker Bell.

"Day one, let's go!" Katie links her arm through mine as we head down the winding maze of corridors.

Liam

Today is 'Get In' day, which is exactly what it sounds like. It's the day when the set arrives at the theatre, the stage crew build the scenery and we arrange all our technical equipment. In the space where the cast would usually be warming up, there are dozens of large speakers being hauled in for the sound crew to check over and assemble as well as lighting rigs and dozens of flight cases.

As instructed by my call sheet, I start setting up the soundboard, and in the silence, I let my mind wander. The argument with Di weighs heavily on my mind and I'm already feeling guilty about the way I spoke to her. Knowing she won't break her silence first, I shoot her a quick apologetic text before I crouch down under the desk and connect the wires.

"I'm sorry too," Di says, startling me. I jump in shock, banging my head on the underside of the desk and, I swear, I can feel Di shaking as she does her best to suppress her laughter.

"Bloody hell, Di. You couldn't announce your presence or something?" I whinge, rubbing the back of my head where it throbs.

"Look, kid—"

"I'm not a kid." I argue, but I guess to her, I always will be.

"Right, sorry, Liam. I'm not going to tell you what you can or can't do or who you can or can't speak to. You're a grown man and I seem to forget that sometimes. And while I'm apologising, I should say sorry for the way I emailed you last night, telling you that you didn't get the promotion you were promised. I should have waited and had the conversation in person."

Without saying anything, I give her a hug, towering over her tiny frame as she wraps her arms around me, patting me on the back.

I pull away and get back to work, but Di doesn't move.

"When was the last time you read your contract?" she asks nonchalantly, but there's something beneath her words that raises my hackles.

"I don't know, it hasn't changed the entire time I've been here. Why?" Now I think about it, I sign a new one for each production we work on and I've never once thought to read it fully, I just assumed that it was always the same.

"You might want to re-read it. I think you'll find it informative. Harriet's contract is the same." Di is still smiling, but it's obviously fake, not quite meeting her eyes anymore. Without another word, she moves to the side, sitting in a seat next to the sound booth so she can work near me. When she picks up her phone and smiles at a text on the screen the hairs on the back of my neck prickle. She's texting Dad.

Dad and I have always had a strained relationship, and that's putting things mildly. He ignored my existence until I was seven. He simply didn't believe that the woman he'd had a one-night stand with could be pregnant, so he turned his back on Mam, leaving her to cope with a new baby on her own.

I don't know what changed his mind, but he turned up on our doorstep one Sunday afternoon with Di and ambushed us, demanding a DNA test. Of course, it came back positive and there began the torture of joint custody, although I don't remember ever staying with him since he lived in London and my life was here in Sunderland.

He was never overly paternal, but when I was sixteen, he gave me my first job here at his family's theatre selling overpriced buckets of popcorn, ice cream and drinks and told me I had to put the money I earned towards my education, because god forbid any son of his wouldn't know what hard work was.

Fourteen years later, I'm still working for him in the most junior position in my field. I know I sound petty and spoiled – my daddy won't give me a promotion, boohoo – but I've worked so hard for him for years and not once has he ever said 'good job, son'.

I hate that I want his validation so much.

"Come on, kid. It's time for the meeting," Di says before I

can dwell on my thoughts too much.

People file into the auditorium where the show's director, Robert, always holds his meetings.

Robert is a tall man with narrow shoulders and long black hair pulled back into a ponytail. His pale complexion and Gothic dress sense remind me of Noel Fielding. The cast gather around him where he perches on the edge of the stage, letting his feet dangle into the orchestra pit, which is a health and safety nightmare waiting to happen.

That's when I spot Harriet.

Across the room, she's talking animatedly to Katie. I can tell she's excited – her hair bounces around her face having already escaped from her messy bun.

"Ugh," Di says as an urgent message comes through her radio from stage door. "Get yourself over there and I'll catch you in a bit." She dashes off, leaving me on my own.

CHAPTER SIX

Harriet

Last week I met most of the crew at the studio but this morning the place is bustling with more unfamiliar faces, some that work for the production and others that work for the theatre.

I casually look around, trying my best not to make it obvious I'm looking for someone specific.

I can't see Liam at first but then an invisible force drags my attention to the back of the auditorium where he stands by the sound booth. He is talking to Diana who turns on her heel and races off somewhere, and then without looking around, his eyes meet mine.

When he smiles at me, I can feel my blush creeping up my neck. I return his smile and look away shyly, turning back to Katie who is grinning excitedly.

"What?" I pretend I have no idea why she's looking at me so intently.

"I take it you've met Liam?"

"We ran into each other this morning, quite literally. My bum still hurts from hitting the pavement," I explain, waving the whole thing off.

She looks over my shoulder to where he stands, making it obvious that we're talking about him.

"Seems like you made quite the impression on him. He's coming over."

"Stop making it obvious that we're talking about him," I hiss.

Shaking her head with a laugh, Katie takes a seat and pulls me down next to her, leaving one seat free on the aisle that Liam takes.

"Good morning, Katherine," he says, addressing his cousin formally, which makes her roll her eyes and cough the word 'loser' into her hand. "Harriet, nice to see you again," he adds to me, his voice smooth and low.

"Hi." I give a little wave in his direction and internally cringe at my lack of coolness.

"Welcome, welcome, everyone settle down please," Robert booms, making the entire auditorium fall silent. I swear even the cleaners all the way in the upper circle vacuum a little quieter as a result. "I trust you all found your dressing rooms okay this morning?"

A murmur of agreement spreads throughout the crowd as Liam and I glance towards each other and Robert gives us the standard introductory safety talk.

"So, this is it," he says. "Day One at The Whitton Theatre, Sunderland. As you can see the main elements of the set are ready for our first show on Tuesday night. The theatre has graciously let us come in five days prior to show day to rehearse on stage with the full set, so that's what we'll be doing for the next few days. I trust you've checked your call sheets for the day so I'm sure I don't need to go through that. So, without further ado, let's get this show on the road!" he concludes with a loud clap of his hands. There's a rumble in the auditorium as everyone stands, their seats flipping up and hitting the backrests, chatting as they leave. Liam looks like he's about to say something to us but is interrupted by Diane for the second time this morning.

"Liam," she commands calmly, and Katie's face hardens ever so slightly as though she's trying hard not to show what she really thinks. To say my curiosity is piqued is an understatement.

"Have a fun morning, ladies," he says with a tight-lipped smile, before walking back towards Diane.

"Let's go, I want to get a good spot to warm up," Katie says, her expression normal again as we make our way to the dress circle bar where we'll be warming up today.

When we arrive, people are already stretching. We aren't a large cast, there are fifteen of us altogether, but the room looks full. There are cast members with their legs propped up on the brass handrail along the bar as if it's a ballet barre and others in all kinds of positions against walls and on the floor.

We find a spot next to Zach, the third and final newbie in our tight-knit friendship group. He is playing the lead role, the hero of our story, but this is his first role on stage for over ten years. He's been brought in as star power and although I don't tend to agree with stunt casting in the theatre, Zach began his career on stage before making a name for himself in TV dramas and has slotted back into theatre life well.

Having him here is a big deal and has brought a lot of

attention to the production, which the company loves, of course.

Zach smiles as we join him and the three of us work our way through our stretching routines, chatting as we go from various positions to pass the time. Every now and then I spot Liam, usually standing across the room chatting to our dance captain while looking at the iPad and clipboard in his arms.

When we're done, Katie turns to me and says, "That was some slow stretching today, Harriet. Any particular reason?" She bumps her hip against mine with a knowing grin.

Okay, when Liam was around, maybe I did stretch a little more seductively than normal, it doesn't mean anything though. At least, that's what I'm telling myself.

"He's single, you know," she says, raising her eyebrows comically.

"I'm not looking for romance," I say with conviction.

"Even with Liam?" Zach says, not believing a single word that comes out of my mouth. "He could win a Henry Cavill lookalike competition and you'd say no? Even I can see he's a good-looking guy and I'm straight. I'm pretty sure any girl on this production wants to be noticed by him."

"Except me," Katie adds.

"Like I said, I'm not looking for romance."

"You don't need to be looking for romance for romance to find you," Zach says poetically.

"Okay, Romeo." I pat his shoulder. "Settle down."

One thing I've learned about Zach is that he's a true romantic and isn't afraid to show it, which was surprising paired with his bad boy, womanising reputation.

"He's not wrong," Katie says, siding with him.

"Well done, guys," Robyn, our dance captain, says, thankfully freeing me from this conversation, and everyone stops what they're doing to turn to her. "Okay, we're going to have a quick break and then come back for vocal warm-ups. After that, we're going to fit your mics and make sure everyone is comfortable before sound check this afternoon. See you all back here in ten minutes."

CHAPTER SEVEN
Harriet

Following a brief break to get some water, we complete our vocal warm-ups and head out to the sound booth for our mic fitting.

Looking around the empty auditorium I can picture the crowd sitting there, waiting in anticipation for the show to start. Chills tremble up my spine as I think about it. Even in the few short hours since our cast and crew meeting this morning, the stage crew have transformed the stage from a cavernous black space into something beginning to look like our set.

"Harriet," Liam calls out my name, smiling as I walk towards him to get my mic fitted.

I don't speak as he works methodically around me, instead I listen and absorb his gravelly voice as he instructs me how to do this myself in the future. Not that I don't already know this, but I'm enraptured nonetheless. My breath hitches at the contact when he passes the mic belt around my waist to fasten at the front. I know he hears it and instead of working quickly like he did with the other actors, he slows his pace, bringing his eyes up to meet mine as the buckle clicks in place.

Still close to me, he reaches to the table next to us to grab the mic. He hooks and moulds the wire over my left ear first. When he brushes a few wisps of baby hairs out of the way, the rough pads of his fingers leave a trail of heat in their wake and the feeling zaps my entire body.

"Could you turn around and bend your neck forward please?" He brushes my hair out of the way as I reluctantly turn away from him, my knees unsteady. Christ, I've known this man all of five minutes and my body is responding in ways it really shouldn't be.

I lift my hand to hold my hair, our fingers brushing as he adjusts my positioning ever so slightly, letting out a chuckle as the shorter wisps at the nape of my neck spring back to their original position.

My breathing is shallow as I try to concentrate on the table covered in microphones instead of how it feels to be touched by him. I count them and try to regain a shred of composure, but it's hard when a man as attractive as Liam is literally standing behind me and stroking me. All I can think of is how those calloused hands would feel on the rest of my body as I bend further over this table.

Shit.

"Almost done," he says quietly, and the throbbing between my legs intensifies. I wonder if this is affecting him as much as it is me. My question is answered immediately when he attaches the pack to the mic belt resting against my bare back. His body is tense as he uses two hands to slide the belt into a better position on my waist, his fingers gripping me as if he's trying not to react but when I risk a glance over my shoulder and our eyes meet in this intimate position, there's a darkness that could only be desire in his eyes.

Holy shit, I feel like I'm in the intro to a stagey porno and he's about to take me roughly in the sound booth. This is one of the most erotic moments of my life and all he's doing is fitting my mic.

Using his hands that are still holding my waist, he turns me to face him again so he can check the positioning of the mic, and I shiver when he touches my cheek again.

"Did I do something wrong?" he asks in a nervous whisper too low for anyone else to hear.

"No, not at all." My voice is hoarse, and I have to clear my throat. I'm not even embarrassed because now that Liam is facing me, I can see the spark in his eyes that tells me he's pleased with my reaction to him.

When he offers me his final nod of approval, I thank him softly and make my way from the wings to the stage where Zach and Katie are waiting patiently for their turn.

Rachael, the principal lead and star of the show, stops dead in front of me on her way to get her mic fitted by Liam too.

"Are you okay, hun? You look a little… green." Her voice is high pitched and though she may sound concerned, she has a catty glint in her eye that says otherwise.

"I'm fine." I move to pass by her, but she moves too, blocking me.

"I wouldn't waste your time, Harriet, he's unavailable. And he doesn't date actresses."

There's bitterness in her words and understanding dawns on me. "Ah good job you warned me," I say sarcastically, before walking away. The last thing I need is to get into a cat fight on day one.

Sound check on get in day is a long, repetitive process. After the cast finish, the band completes theirs, so we move back to the dress circle bar so we're not in the way. It's more relaxed at the end of the day since we're all so exhausted. We spend the time waiting to run through more lines together, some of us work on choreography and others are recording TikTok videos.

As much as I feel like a walking zombie when I leave that evening, I perk up when I see Liam in the hallway chatting to one of the band. She flicks her hair and bats her eyelashes, but Liam doesn't seem to notice her blatant flirting. I wonder if this happens to him a lot, first the stage door keeper, then Rachael and now this, it's like the guy is a magnet for sexy women.

"Goodnight," I say to them both and turn sideways to squeeze past them in the narrow hallway not wanting to interrupt. It's none of my business if Liam gets hit on, I have to tell myself for the umpteenth time today.

"Hey, Harriet, wait a second," Liam calls out, jogging to catch up with me. "How was your day? You looked like you were having fun." His dimples appear when he smiles at me again.

"Have you been watching me?" I narrow my eyes, teasing him flirtatiously as we wander through the same corridors as this morning.

"Oh god, not in a creepy way or anything, like, I saw you and thought you looked great and I'm…" Understanding dawns on him. "You were joking, right… uh well…" he adds, looking down to pick imaginary fluff from his black polo shirt like he's trying to think of something else to say.

Is… is he nervous?

"I had a fantastic day. Thank you for noticing." I put him out of his misery, even though seeing him flustered might be my new favourite thing.

"A few of us are going for dinner and a drink down at The Stack tonight, are you coming?"

"Not tonight, I've got to get home." As much as I'd love to change my plans to hang out with him, I'm dying to get home and tell Dad all about my day.

"Maybe next time?"

I nod in agreement, noticing we've reached the exit already and disappointment washes over me that today is over.

"I'll see you tomorrow then, I actually have to go back" – he points his thumb over his shoulder down the corridor – "but I wanted to say goodnight before you left."

I bend down and sign myself out while Liam grabs the door and holds it open for me.

"Have a good night, Liam." I give him a regretful smile.

"Yeah, I will… You too."

CHAPTER EIGHT
Liam

The Stack is a leisure venue built out of old shipping containers on the Seaburn seafront not too far from our theatre, so we head there after we're done for the day. There is a large communal courtyard in the centre on the lower level, which acts as the main seating area partially covered by sails, as well as an upper-level balcony that houses more seats looking out over the courtyard on one side and out to sea on the other.

Usually, the fire pits and patio heaters would be lit but since we're in the middle of a heatwave, the usual smell of burning wood makes way for the scent of delicious street food.

Zach, Katie and I are the first to arrive, so Katie saves us a seat at one of the long bench tables made from repurposed steel pipes and wood while Zach and I weave through the courtyard to the bar.

He's a good guy, Zach. We go way back, all the way to drama school, and we've kept in touch ever since, although this is the first time our paths have crossed professionally since he's been trapped in TV land. Zach is the only one, apart from Katie and Di, who knows who my dad is.

We make small talk as we order and wait for our drinks,

and it feels like no time has passed since our teenage years.

"You okay, man?" he asks, sensing the air of melancholy surrounding me as we walk back to our table drinks in hand.

"Is there anything in your contract preventing you from dating anyone from the company?" I ask, knowing this conversation won't go anywhere beyond us and Katie.

Once I walked Harriet out tonight, Diane's ominous comments about contracts played on my mind. I walked back to my dressing room and pulled up my contract on my laptop, and there it was in black and white.

Section 7.3 – Romantic Relationships: The employee is not permitted to engage in romantic relationships in the workplace with cast, crew or any other Whitton Group employee. Any romantic relationship with a third party that classifies as a conflict of interest should be disclosed at the earliest opportunity. Failure to comply will result in a breach of contract and could result in loss of employment.

"No, not that I know of. Is there one in yours?"

"Yeah, and, it's a sackable offence if I break it. I'd never noticed it before, because, well…" I trail off not wanting to go too deep. "It's not just that," I add, quickly moving on. "There are more differences in my contract this year compared to previous. Like, if I voluntarily leave the production before the end of my employment, I can't work for a rival company or theatre for six months and I can't conduct any self-employed work in the theatre industry while I'm working here as it's a conflict of interest."

"But loads of us offer workshops and classes while we tour.

It's how we pay the bills."

"I know."

"What are you going to do then?" Zach asks as we join Katie at the table.

"What are you going to do about what?" she asks.

While Zach pulls his contract up on his phone, I quickly relay the information to Katie who is just as puzzled.

"There's none of this in mine," Zach confirms.

"Can you talk to your dad? Surely, he can get it changed. I mean, they seem like extremely unfair conditions," Katie suggests.

"My dad is the one who wrote my contract."

Neither Katie or Zach seem surprised by this even though their contracts were likely written by a random HR person.

"Do you want to do any of those things in your contract?" Zach asks. "Do workshops, move to another company, ask someone out on a date?"

I roll my eyes at him, knowing exactly where he's going with this.

"There was a spark between me and Harriet when we met, and she seems like someone I'd like to get to know better. But I don't know, I only met her today, so it seems a little presumptuous to assume if I did want to ask her out she'd say yes."

"She seemed pretty set against the idea of a workplace romance earlier," Katie says, and it stings. Even though I can't sacrifice my career to ask her out, I thought the attraction was mutual.

"Come on, did you not see the way she reacted when he

mic'd her up today. It was so romantic and intimate. There's definitely attraction from both sides," Zach debates with Katie, neither of them bothering to even glance my way.

"Yeah, that chemistry was better than porn. But just because they're attracted to one another doesn't mean he should risk his career pursuing something Harriet has told us she doesn't want."

"You really believe her?" Zach questions her.

"You guys know I'm still here, right?"

"It's a shame she couldn't make it tonight," Zach says thoughtfully.

"Her dad has cancer so she's helping her mam and sister take care of him at home. From what she said, her dad doesn't have long left." Katie's comments transport me back in time to when I cared for my mam through her final battle with cancer. Night-time was the worst, too terrified to sleep in case something happened, but too tired, emotionally and physically, to make her last few weeks with me worthwhile. Instead, most of the time we sat in silence together.

"I'm sorry," Katie says. "I know it must be tough to hear."

"It's fine, I just wish I could do something for her," I say.

"We need to give her a little stability, don't you think? The new job, the move back from London and her dad's illness, that's a lot of stressful change she's been through in such a short time," Katie says, and Zach and I nod in agreement.

Shortly after, our conversation is interrupted by Rachael and some of the other cast and crew, so we swiftly move on to safer topics.

For the next two hours, Rachael dominates the conversation about some publicity thing she's been offered down in London. She seems really excited about it. From what I gather, she's been asked to represent the production company in a photo shoot and a recorded performance of a few of the songs from the show. If you ask me, agreeing to take time away in tech week is cutting it fine, but if the company has approved it so close to opening night, it must be worth it.

"You're not drinking tonight, Liam?" Rachael asks, coming to sit next to me with a swish of her waist-length platinum hair.

"Not tonight, I'm driving."

"Oh, boooo! Leave the car here and get it tomorrow. We can deal with the hangover when you wake up," she says, in a playful attempt at flirting.

"My thirty-year-old hangover hits differently to your twenty-three-year-old hangover, believe me." I aim for a joke although it's true.

Holding onto my forearm, she pouts and bats her eyelashes. "Is hanging out with me not worth it?" My eyes drop to her fingertips, clinging onto me like talons, and I have to work really hard not to flinch away from her. She has worked with our production company for a couple of years now and every time we work together, she tries this, no matter how many times I've told her it's inappropriate and that I'm not interested.

"Liam, can you take me home now?" Katie asks,

materialising from nowhere, and I'm so thankful for the rescue.

"Yes!" I say a little too enthusiastically, and I don't miss the side-eye Rachael shoots Katie.

I smile apologetically at Rachael even though I'm not sorry at all, and thankfully we leave without a scene.

When I finally get home, I turn my shower onto the coldest setting and step under the powerful spray, letting the water pressure knead some of the tension from my shoulders.

Now that I'm home and have time to process the day, it's obvious that Di was keeping me busy on purpose, she's never worked me so hard and I'm starting to feel it already.

Despite Di's best efforts, a stroke of luck brought Harriet to me for her mic fitting and I've not stopped thinking about it since. The chemistry I felt with her this morning could have been an anomaly, some elevated emotion brought on by my morning jog, but this afternoon it was like it had multiplied tenfold. She's like forbidden fruit and I'm Adam wanting a bite of that apple. You better believe I'll be fitting her mic every day from now on just to prove it really happened.

I scroll Instagram to pass the time until I fall asleep and come across a photo that Katie posted of her and Harriet from earlier today that makes me sit bolt upright. I know I've got it bad when I spend far too long looking at her bright green-blue eyes. Her smile is so pure it's contagious and I can't help but smile back.

Thanking my lucky stars that Harriet is tagged, I click on her name, which takes me straight to her profile.

Harriet Adams

MT-Swing @LoveEverAfter UK Tour

Graduate – London School of Musical Theatre

The first post on her grid was posted a few hours ago. It's a cluster of photos captioned: 'Hell week… Feels like heaven week' with an angel emoji and a pink love heart. The first is a picture of her alone standing outside of the theatre, the golden rays of the sunrise giving her an illuminated glow. She's wearing the jogging bottoms and cropped t-shirt she had on when we met. I swipe to look at more pictures and there's another photo of her with Katie and one with Zach. They're having fun; you can see it right there on their faces and I want nothing more than to be a part of that.

I scroll further down her feed, there's a picture of her announcing her part in our show, there are a lot of photos of her standing outside various West End Theatres, some from when she worked on the West End and a few pictures of Harriet and people I assume are her friends. There's something different about these pictures though. The only ones that match the shine in her eyes from first photo are the ones where she's standing with her sister or her family.

A picture of a bubble bath complete with candles and a romance book titled Love and London, posted half an hour ago, pops up when I click on her stories. Another photo follows of her silky smooth, wet legs peeking out from the bubbles that makes my mouth go dry and all the blood in my body rush south. The text bubble on the picture says 'Instagram' followed by the next photo with the word 'reality'. She has a messy bun on her head, bubbles

53

up to her chin and a mud mask on her face. She's pulling a funny face at the camera, her eyes are crossed and her tongue is sticking out, and I laugh out loud at her infectious humour. Seeing how cute she is makes me all warm inside until I remember what Katie told me about her dad.

These happy pictures are likely a mask hiding what she's really going through, something I know all too well and wouldn't wish on my own worst enemy.

When Mam was sick, it almost killed me to watch her suffer but I never let her or anyone else see that. I would cry on my own in the shower where no one could hear or see my tears, where my bloodshot eyes could be excused by simply getting soap in them.

Is that what Harriet is doing now?

A second after the thought runs through my mind, a notification pops up on the screen.

@IamHarrietAdams is now following you.

CHAPTER NINE
Harriet

"So how did today go?" Jayne asks through the crack in the bathroom door. She's sitting on the landing next to the gap with her back pressed against the wall as I soak in the bath. I lasted all of five minutes alone with my thoughts before I called for her to come and keep me company.

"Tiring, of course, but it felt amazing to be back."

"Are you ready to talk about whatever has you so distracted tonight?" Of course, Jayne has noticed I'm distracted. The whole car journey home all I could think about was how lucky I am to have been given a second chance at my career and how I promised myself I would never put myself in a position where history could repeat itself.

"Harriet?" she prompts when I don't respond.

"I met someone today."

"You met someone? Like, a guy?"

"Yeah."

After a long beat of silence, she almost loses her temper. "Oh, for the love of god, please continue this story," she says on a long, excited exhale. "Is he sexy?"

The words tumble out of me as I tell her all about Liam,

how we met in the street and the insane chemistry between us.

"I know he felt it too, it was there in his eyes, as if I could see the fire burning in them."

"So... What's the problem?"

"I don't know, it... it felt quick. I'm not sure I believe in love at first sight, but, like, intense sexual and emotional chemistry at first sight for sure. I wanted to... I don't know, nibble on him or stick my tongue down his throat and do obscenely filthy things to him all day."

My confession doesn't shock my sister. Jayne and I have always been open about sex and relationships, I guess you have a unique bond when you go through puberty at the same time. What isn't fun is when your periods sync and you take your teenage hormonal rage out on each other.

Luckily for us, we grew out of that.

"Woah!" She laughs, and although I can't see her face, I know her eyes will be as wide as saucers. "It's been a while since I've heard you this passionate about a man." She pretends to be scandalised.

"I know what I had with Chris was superficial because I never felt like this about him, I never looked at him and thought 'I want to rip your clothes off' and when we broke up, I wasn't upset. I was embarrassed by the way it ended and how I was so naive that I couldn't see what was right in front of me."

"Chris was a prick. What's the problem with Liam though?"

"I can't date him." I let my fingers glide through the water, watching the ripples as they float away from the sway of my hand. "I make one mistake and I get a reputation."

"Be more specific."

"They wrote a clause in my contract forbidding any romantic relationship with cast and/or crew. Otherwise, my contract will be terminated."

"Ah."

"Yeah," I say thoughtfully, knowing there's nothing else to say. I won't ruin my career twice by making the same mistake.

"It wasn't your fault, Harriet," Jayne's words cut through the thick silence.

"I got myself into that situation, I can't blame anyone else."

"You were forced into a vulnerable position by someone you trusted," she says, defending me when I won't defend myself.

"Regardless of who is to blame, it happened, and I need to make sure it doesn't happen again." I try my best to convince myself.

"Okay. Stay away from this Liam guy and be done with it." She makes it sound so simple.

I can totally do that. Tomorrow morning, I'll go to work. I'll not flirt with the man, hell, I won't even look at him.

Jayne and I sit in a comfortable silence for a while, listening to the distant beeping sounds of Dad's machines in the other room.

"Harriet?"

"Yeah?"

"I missed this while you were in London."

My heart swells. "Me too."

"When Dad moves to the hospice, I think I'll come visit you on tour. We've not had a good night out together in such a long time."

"I'd love that. You've done so much for Dad; you deserve a break." Guilt bubbles from deep within me, she's been here all this time and hasn't complained once about caring for Dad. All I've really done since I came home with my tail between my legs is wallow in my own self-pity.

"How are you coping, Jayne?" I ask for the first time.

"Oh, as fine as I can be. It's tough, seeing him like this. But then he smiles at me and I sort of forget for a second. On a morning when he wakes up and I bring him a cup of tea and he looks at me with so much love. When I come home and show him some of the photos I've taken, either at the studio or when I've been out with Wearside Football Club, he can't help but beam with pride, it makes the tiredness worth it." Her answer might be true, but it's also rehearsed.

"Is that really how you feel? You can talk to me, you don't need to put on a brave face."

She lets out a shaky breath. "I have good days and bad days. On the bad days, all I want to do is have him nap so I can cry without worrying he'll see me. On the really bad days…" Her voice is barely above a whisper, uneven with emotion, and I wish I could take away her guilt for feeling this way. "I want to run away from it all. Does that make me a bad person?"

"It makes you human," I try to sound reassuring but when she sniffs back her tears, I see how much pressure she is truly under.

Even though she's the baby of the family, she's always been the more mature of the two of us, more put together and sensible. Where I've never really had a proper job, even when I was a teenager, Jayne had a part-time job throughout college. She opened her own photography studio when she was eighteen because she had saved all her wages as well as birthday and Christmas money since she was ten years old.

It never occurred to me that she has been struggling because she's always so strong and resilient.

I climb out of the bath and wrap a towel around me, tucking it in at the front. I leave a trail of bubbles in my wake as I open the door fully and sit down on the landing carpet next to my little sister.

"Hey." I wrap my arm around her and she cuddles into my side, letting out a sob. "I'm here, we'll get through this together. Even when I'm not here in the flesh, I'm always at the other end of the phone. I'm your big sister, I'll love you until my last breath and I'll never judge you for the way you're feeling because I know your wonderful heart better than I know my own."

She lets out another sob in response, so I squeeze her tighter.

"Do you want to sleep in my room tonight?" I ask and she nods. When we were kids and one of us would have a nightmare or there was a thunderstorm, we'd always sleep together. Jayne said it was because she knew I needed comfort but looking back, I think she needed me more than she let on.

Once we're both dressed for bed, Jayne comes into my room carrying her pillow and the cuddly cat called Kitty I bought her when she was born. It's threadbare and has a grey tinge instead of the brilliant white colour it once was.

"Right, let's see a picture of this Liam." She jumps into my bed and pulls on the covers. "Is he on social media?"

"I'm not sure, let's check Instagram," I say, unlocking my phone. I click on my stories first to check the views, and there he is, right at the top of the list.

He's viewed my story.

"What?" Jayne asks as I stare blankly at his name on the screen.

"I uh, I think he's looked me up on Instagram. I can see that he's viewed my stories and I'm sure you can only see stories if you follow or search for that person."

I click on the profile and his life according to a three-by-three grid appears in front of me.

"Let me see!"

I hand her my phone and she scrolls through his profile. "He's not your usual type. He literally looks like Thor if Chris Hemsworth had dark hair. I mean, look at those arms and shoulders, looks like he could toss you around like a ragdoll." She smiles and clicks something on the screen. "There, you can have it back now." Her expression is obviously mischievous, she might as well have a big glowing sign above her that reads 'meddling little sister'!

"What did you do?" I ask, but I needn't have, it's right there as I look at the screen.

"I followed him for you." She grins.

"What the hell, Jayne! He's going to think I'm weird or

something for following him when we've just met."

Tossing my phone to the bottom of my bed, I dive beneath my pillow with an embarrassed groan.

"He was the one looking at your stories of you in the bath." She laughs as she lifts the pillow from my face. "That would make him the weird one."

I start to protest but then my phone chimes with an Instagram notification. I dart out from beneath my pillow, throwing it across the room, looking at Jayne in alarm. We both dive to the bottom of my bed where my phone lies, but she beats me to it.

"That was quick. Must be keen." Jayne is unable to keep the grin off her face.

I grab my phone from her and stare at it in giddy disbelief.

@TheWrightLiam is now following you.

CHAPTER TEN
Liam

The next morning, I arrive at work early.

Di seems both shocked and pleased to see me ready and eager to go and I'm relieved to start my day with no arguments. The set is fully assembled now, as are sound and props, so today's job is getting the lighting rigs installed ready for the first tech run tomorrow. The army of people in the wardrobe and wig department are buzzing around getting the quick-change wardrobe village set up at the back of the stage behind the set and checking for any repairs needed on the costumes, so I make myself scarce.

"I'll drop these call sheets off at the dressing rooms before the cast arrive," I shout across the stage at Cory, the deputy stage manager, and he nods in acknowledgement.

It doesn't take much time for me to clip the sheets to the noticeboards outside the dressing rooms and in the green room, so I make it to stage door a little earlier than intended. A few of the cast and crew pass and say good morning as I wait on the low wall outside, enjoying the way the sun warms my face. I explain to those who ask that I'm getting a little fresh air, and I tell myself that this is completely normal behaviour and not at all weird.

"Good morning," I say when Harriet rounds the corner and comes into view, rewarding me with her bright infectious smile.

"Good morning." She comes to a halt in front of me as I stand. Her voice is low and a little hoarse, as if she's not used it much this morning. "Are you waiting for me?"

"I was on my phone, and you know what the signal is like in there," I explain, not wanting to creep her out. I don't think she believes me, but she plays along anyway. "I'm heading back in there now so I'll walk with you."

"Sounds great. And look at us, not causing physical injury to each other this morning." She playfully bumps her hip against mine as we walk towards the door, her eyes twinkling. "We're getting so good at this."

"Are you hurt? After yesterday I mean." A wave of guilt ripples over me at the reminder of our tumble yesterday.

"No." Her laugh is soft and gentle. "I'm teasing, I'm perfectly fine. Are you?" She pats my chest as she slides past me through the door I'm holding open for her, and I can feel the warmth of her touch through my thin t-shirt.

Am I fine? Let me think? I'm currently inches from the girl who's been running through my mind constantly for the past twenty-four hours. We're standing so close I can smell her fruity shampoo and she just touched my chest in a way that has my heart racing.

"Yeah." My voice has a slight tremble to it, but I recover quickly so I don't think she notices. "I'm totally fine. I was concerned I'd hurt you."

It's a much cooler morning today, Harriet is wearing black sweatpants and a baggy hoodie and although she's covered up, I can't stop thinking about what she looks like under there after seeing her warming up in her leotard and leggings yesterday. I know how toned and nimble her body is and I also know how smooth and silky her legs are after the photo of her in the bath.

And…now I'm picturing her in the bath like some sort of degenerate.

Fuck.

Checking the time on her watch, she signs in on the clipboard attached to the wall. We make small talk about the day's schedule as we walk through the green room to the corridor leading to the dressing rooms. As we make our way down the narrow corridor, her soft hand brushes against mine sending sparks crackling between us. She glances up at me with a shy smile and when I bump my shoulder playfully against hers a pink blush spreads across her cheeks.

We come to a stop outside her dressing room, but she doesn't move to open the door, instead we stand facing each other.

"Did you know that Elphaba in *Wicked* was named after the author of *The Wizard of Oz*, L. Frank Baum?" she asks randomly.

I sound out the words, "El-pha-ba. L. Frank Baum… Oh my god, you're right. I didn't know that. Do you have any other cool facts?"

"I don't think I'd class them as cool." She looks away with a hint of self-deprecation in her voice.

"I would."

Her smile returns. "Why don't you wait outside for me again tomorrow morning and I'll give you another fact then?" she suggests with a smile as she backs into her dressing room, not taking her eyes off me. She leaves the door open and takes a seat at her dressing table.

I grip the top of the doorframe and lean forward. Exactly like our first encounter yesterday, I can feel the air around pulsing, as though there's an energy between us that I can't see but sure as hell can feel. It's literally pulling my body towards her.

"I definitely will," I say, fuelled by the confidence she injects into me. "See you soon, Harriet." And by some miracle, I manage to pull myself away from her and get back to work.

I don't see Harriet again until later that morning. And technically, I can only hear her. She's just finished a vocal warm-up on stage while I'm checking the prop inventory for the second time in as many days as instructed by Di. It really doesn't need doing again, so I'm quite sure I'm being micromanaged into staying out of the way again.

Maybe she thinks that by separating us I'll get over my crush. Because a crush is exactly what this is, it's not just attraction, I can't get her out of my head at all.

On days like today there is usually a lot of sitting around for the cast as we work around them, tinkering with the set, sound and lighting. Some of the cast use their phones or go on social media, others warm up, run through choreography or sing. Harriet and some of the other cast are singing and hearing them challenge each other to sing songs from other musicals is the only thing making this menial task enjoyable. They're singing their audition songs from their original self-tapes, and I get flashbacks of helping Katie film her version of "Popular" from *Wicked*.

Zach follows Katie with "Louder Than Words" from *Tick, Tick... Boom* and then Rachael sings "No Way" from *Six*.

"What was your self-tape, Harriet?" someone, I'm not exactly sure who, asks, immediately getting my attention.

"'That Would be Enough' from *Hamilton*."

Everyone immediately agrees it's a great song choice for her voice and whoever is controlling the music finds the track quickly.

I hear Zach step in and cover Hamilton's lines in the beginning but when she launches into her song, there is complete silence apart from her angelic voice. Everyone including Robert and Di have stopped to watch, so I drop what I'm doing too, I need to see her.

It's the first time I've heard her sing and I can guarantee that if I wasn't already crushing on her, this performance would have done it.

Instead of emerging from the wings, I head out to the auditorium and take a seat on one of the plush velvet seats to get a better view. She looks so incredibly at ease up on that stage, way more comfortable than I ever was in my performing days in my teens. I had a decent voice, but lacked the confidence to perform in front of an audience.

The words flow seamlessly from her as if the song were written for her specific vocal range, everything about her performance screams perfection and I wonder why on earth she didn't get the lead role instead of swing. Her voice is strong and powerful enough to tackle the big ballads of our show and yet soft enough to take on the softer, sweeter songs too. In this three-minute song she demonstrated her emotional range perfectly matching the emotions of Eliza Hamilton in the original musical.

When she finishes, everyone bursts into a deafening applause, even some of the theatre staff whose offices are hidden just to the side of the dress circle have come out to watch and are all giving her a standing ovation.

Harriet looks surprised, as if she hadn't noticed them before now.

I stand too and when her eyes meet mine, it's like nothing else in this world exists aside from the two of us.

"Well, on that note, I'm leaving for London now," Rachael interrupts in an attempt to get the attention back to her.

"Great news," Robert says. "Have fun and let us know how you get on."

Rachael waves goodbye but people are still fussing over Harriet, which doesn't land well with her, you can almost see her turn green with jealousy.

"Okay, now we're nicely warmed up," Robert continues, "Zach and Harriet, you're going to be singing lead this morning, let's crack on." He claps his hands in his usual commanding way and with it, anyone who isn't meant to be on stage disperses, including me as I begrudgingly make my way back to the prop department in the wings.

CHAPTER ELEVEN

Liam

Just before lunch there's an unexpected knock on my dressing room door.

"Come in," I shout.

The door cracks open and Harriet sticks her head around, looking at the space and noting that I'm alone.

"Hi," I say, pleasantly surprised, and she returns my grin. I close my laptop and put it to the side as she comes into the room, leaving the door open behind her.

"You were incredible this morning."

Her smile widens. "Thank you. I didn't realise you were watching."

"Of course I was, I couldn't tear myself away."

I watch her every movement carefully and silently, committing it all to memory as she walks slowly around the room. There's a copy of *Men's Health* magazine that one of the guys brought in that she picks up from the glass table next to the window and places back down carefully, exactly where she found it.

"Are you jealous of my cool view?" I cut through the silence as she looks out the window at the alley behind the theatre.

"We've got an hour-long lunch break so I thought I would

see if you wanted anything. I was thinking about getting a milkshake from Love Lily," she says, pulling the sleeves of her hoody over her hands.

"That sounds great. I'll come with you. If that's okay?"

"You're not too busy?" She nods at my laptop where I was searching for stage manager jobs a moment ago.

"It can wait." I shrug.

"Let's go."

I grab my wallet and phone from the dressing table that is littered with snacks and drinks, and we head out the door together. Although I know we're not doing anything wrong, we're just getting a milkshake after all, I still check over my shoulder for Di. I can't help but feel like we're sneaking around.

A wall of heat hits us as we exit stage door after being in the air-conditioned venue all morning and the sun streams down onto us from the cloudless blue sky.

"Have you eaten the pancakes at Love Lily before?" I ask as we walk down the steep path towards the sea.

"Oh my god, yes! They're what I imagine dreams taste like," she says with a laugh. "The Galaxy Caramel Brownie ones are my favourite."

"Mine is Cereal Killer. It's the best of both worlds, pancakes and cereal with whatever sauce I feel like on the day." I make a chef's kiss action and she laughs, the sweet tinkle like music to my ears.

"We should come back for pancakes when we have more time. It's a perk of having the theatre at the beach."

"That's a great idea!"

Of course, my body reacts to her enthusiasm. My heart speeds up and my mood feels lighter than it has in such a long time.

There isn't much of a wait at Love Lily when we arrive and place our order. Harriet orders a Nutella milkshake that she informs me is her usual order and I order a Lotus Biscoff iced latte. Our faces are almost pressed against the glass cake cabinet looking at all the delicious bakes as we wait, and then with our drinks in hand, we begin our walk back to the theatre.

"We've got a bit of time; do you fancy a walk along the pier?" I ask, checking my watch before we get to the path that stretches from the promenade to the main road. I'm not ready to end this lunchtime jaunt, and I don't think Harriet is either as she jumps at the chance.

"The sea is really calm today, I bet there's a lovely view."

We take our time walking along the long, cobbled pier towards the lighthouse, sipping on our cold drinks. There are a lot of fishermen milling around, making the most of the warm weather and calm fishing conditions. They take no notice of us, concentrating instead on their task at hand. We walk past buckets and buckets full of crabs and mackerel and Harriet scrunches her nose up at the live bait making me laugh.

When we reach the lighthouse, we walk to the other side facing out to the sea. Harriet shrugs off her cardigan, placing it on the ground at the base of the lighthouse so she can sit on it and motions for me to join her. Today's leotard is backless apart from a few straps that criss cross over her shoulder blades. It gives the perfect view of her toned back muscles and flawless posture.

Leaning back with her legs outstretched in front of her, she tilts her face to the sky and closes her eyes, letting the sun warm her tanned skin as she lets out a content sigh. Her neck is elongated and for a moment I wonder what it would feel like to taste her there. I imagine myself peppering kisses against her soft skin to her jaw as she arches her body towards mine.

"This feels soooo good," she says with a soft moan that sends ripples of desire coursing through me.

"It's different to London that's for sure," I reply, trying to distract myself from the explicit thoughts running through my mind.

"It was one of the biggest things I missed about home. Being able to come to the beach whenever I wanted is something I took for granted before I left." She turns her face to me, squinting against the sunlight. I hand her my sunglasses and pull my cap lower to shield my own eyes. "Thank you," she adds.

"What made you come back?"

"I'd been living in London a long time and I was ready for a change so I auditioned for this musical. When I got the part, it felt like fate. My dad had been diagnosed with bowel and bladder cancer about six months prior and I wanted to come home to be with him. When my agent called with news that the show would be in Sunderland, everything fell into place exactly where I wanted it to."

"I'm sorry to hear about your dad. He must be happy you're home."

"Yeah, he is. He's upset he won't be able to come to the performance though, he has so much medical equipment now, his wheelchair won't even fit in the wheelchair spaces." I can't see her eyes through the sunglasses, but I can hear the sadness behind her words. I want to take it away for her, but I know better than anyone that's impossible.

"I promised I'd send him photos of me in costume, so he'll be thrilled with that." She shrugs.

"Is it terminal?" I ask, already knowing the answer.

She nods. "He's being moved to a hospice as soon as there's a bed ready for him. The pain can get a little much, more so during the night, so it's for the best."

"I'm so sorry, Harriet." I take her hand to comfort her, and she looks down, smiling and squeezing my hand right back. "Do you miss London?" I change the subject. She leans forward to have a drink of her milkshake, breaking the contact between us.

"No," she says matter-of-factly. "It was great when I was young and just starting out because I got to network and meet people in the industry but my last job kind of soured the whole West End experience for me. I can't really say too much about what happened."

"It seemed to work out for you in the end. You fit in so well here with everyone, it feels like you've been here the whole time," I say, trying to reassure her that no matter what happened in London, she belongs here. And I mean it. In the encounters we've had both alone and with the rest of the group, she's slotted in perfectly.

"Thank you, that means more than you know. I've never felt like I fit in before. I was never nerdy enough for the theatre nerds and not cool enough for the cool theatre kids. I guess that's why I'm determined to make sure nothing gets in the way of this job. I almost lost everything in London because I wanted to fit in, I became someone I didn't recognise and trusted the wrong person. I've promised myself I won't risk that here." She stands abruptly, ending the conversation. "Shall we head back to the theatre?"

"Sure," I say, noticing the shift in her demeanour as we slowly make our way back to the shoreline, the easy-going conversation we shared on the walk out here feels stilted now, like a shield has come up between us. When we eventually approach her dressing room door, she hands me back my sunglasses and when she enters the room, she says, "goodbye," with a small smile, closing the door behind her.

CHAPTER TWELVE
Harriet

After our lunchtime walk yesterday, despite me ending it on a slightly awkward note, I spent the afternoon being drawn to Liam like a moth to a flame. I couldn't help myself, I could sense when he was around without having to look until eventually our gazes collided like magnets, an unspoken attraction passing through the air between us.

Despite the alarm bell ringing in my head, saying I should keep Liam firmly in the 'friend from work' box, I can't deny it felt good to have a friend to hang out with, someone who doesn't know about or judge me by my past. I enjoyed his company too, and I do want to see more of him but if I'm going to do that, I need to learn how to keep him in that box I've created.

"Good morning," he says when I reach him. Just like yesterday, he's sitting on the brick wall outside of stage door and just like yesterday my heart flutters in my chest when he stands to face me.

"Good morning," I echo merrily, his smile is contagious.

He holds open the door and gestures to me to go ahead. As usual, I sign in and wave at Stage Door Steph and then we head on through the double doors to the green room. Instead of making our way straight to my dressing room, we take a seat on the worn brown leather couches facing the big TV.

I haven't spent much time here but I'm sure I'll get settled in soon enough. Part of my job as a swing includes a lot of sitting around during shows, waiting in case I'm needed, so thankfully this room is well equipped. There are vending machines and bookshelves packed full of all kinds of books. There is a worn pool table that looks like it's been well loved by many cast and crew and a retro Pac-Man game in the corner.

"You promised me another fact and I'm here to make sure you deliver," he says, his serious tone not quite matching his easy-going grin.

"Okay." Buying myself some thinking time, I make myself comfortable, folding one leg up underneath me as I turn my body towards him. He mirrors me, placing a long arm on the back of the sofa. Our knees bump together, and I'm momentarily distracted by the spark of electricity our contact causes.

"You probably know this one since you've worked here before, but two seats are kept permanently open at this theatre for the ghosts to enjoy whatever is showing," I tell him.

He smiles. "That's quite nice, isn't it?"

"I think so."

"Do you know the names of the ghosts?" Liam asks, and I shake my head urging him to continue his story. "Nancy is a twelve-year-old Victorian girl who is said to have died during a ballet performance when part of the original stage collapsed. She's a playful ghost and likes to play harmless tricks on the crew. And then we have Ralph who was a security guard here in World War Two, he was too old to go abroad to fight so stayed here to protect the people who sought refuge in the theatre after losing their homes. The story goes that a bomb hit part of our dressing room block as he was ushering people into the basement where they'd be safe. He dove in front of a mother and her two young children, protecting them from some of the debris. He saved them but was killed as a result."

"That's so sad, and incredibly selfless of him." An emotional lump lodges itself in my throat.

Liam nods. "His portrait hangs in the bar next to the stalls, he liked to stop for a drop of brandy after a show had cleared out, so it seemed like a fitting location to honour him. There's also an open bottle of brandy left on the top shelf for him."

"Have you ever seen the ghosts?"

"I've never spotted either ghost, but a few of the lighting guys swear they heard Nancy laughing in the gallery as they were setting up the spotlights yesterday afternoon," he says, and it sounds perfectly reasonable given her playful nature.

I give a dramatic shiver and Liam laughs his hearty laugh, lightening the sombre mood.

"If you do come across a ghost, legend has it that they are very friendly and mean no harm," he reassures me. "They're just as excited to be here as we are."

"The Sunderland Empire was also damaged in an air raid," I say, referencing the large theatre in the city centre. "The bomb hit where the Fire Station Cultural Venue is now, which was where the most damage was, but shrapnel and debris damaged the main foyer of their theatre, there's still damage and dents in the brass banisters to this day."

He's grinning at me and I can't help but return it. "What?" I ask.

"I'm just thinking that this is quickly becoming my favourite part of the day."

"I should really get to my dressing room." I quickly stand before I do something stupid like kiss him.

When we arrive at my door I spin around and stop abruptly to face him. I'm flustered and lose my balance, landing with my palms flat against his solid chest.

The air around us trembles. I quickly remove my hands and take a step back, putting some much-needed space between us.

"This is my favourite time of the day too," I say in a breathless rush he probably won't understand.

He smiles at me and nods, stroking down my arm. "Same time tomorrow then?" he asks, and I nod, unable to draw my eyes from him as my breathing stutters.

By one in the afternoon, fatigue is setting in with the entire cast and crew. It's been a long morning on our first tech run, there was a lot of stopping and starting while things were adjusted and re-run.

As there is no sign of Rachael returning today, I had to step in to run through her track as well as covering my own for my ensemble role, which is exhausting in itself. In some cases, throughout the tech run, entire scene changes are to be made and when the creative team go back to the drawing board for the fourth time today, Robert sends us all out for lunch.

I check my phone on the walk back to our dressing room and grin when I find an Instagram message from Liam asking if I'd like to join him for another lunchtime stroll.

"I'm heading out for lunch with Liam," I say to Katie as I pick up my purse from the dressing table. "Do you want anything?"

"Two lunch dates in a row? Are things getting serious?" she jokingly asks.

"We're just getting to know each other as friends. Lord knows I could use more of them since moving back here. We have a lot in common with theatre stuff too, I enjoy talking to him, you know?" I explain, although I'm sure Katie sees right through me.

"Well, I hope you have fun, I'm going to have a steam, I need it," she says, prepping her Nelson's steamer on the dressing table. She leans over and flicks on our travel kettle, so I leave her to it and make my way to his dressing room.

What I said to Katie is true, I don't have many friends. Besides Katie and Zach – who are relatively new in my life, but I already know I can't live without them – I've only got my sister Jayne, everyone else in London sort of… disappeared after everything that happened.

Liam's room is empty when I arrive, so I take a seat and try my best not to snoop.

I give in, I'm totally snooping.

I'm sitting in the chair marked with his name and look around, there are a few personal care items like deodorant and aftershave that I spritz in the air, taking a deep inhale of the familiar aroma. The woody, citrus scent takes me right back to the day we met, and I'm sucked into the memory of him lying on top of me in the street, his hard body pressing against mine, and the way he looked at me so intently, so deeply until we came to our senses and my embarrassment set in.

I lean back in his chair, propping my feet up on the footrest and close my eyes as I picture the scene. He looks at me the same way when I'm talking to him as he did that first day, as if he's transfixed by every word that comes out of my mouth. I wonder if he would be the same if he ever kissed me? Would he look at me like that as he slowly and thoroughly worships my body and brings me to the brink of pleasure? Yeah, I think he would.

I let my mind wander down a filthy path, imagining all the delicious things I'd want him to do to me even though allowing myself to fantasise about this is a bad idea.

"Sorry, I got held up for a sec," he says. I jump out of his seat, shocked right out of my X-rated daydreams. I'm still gripping the bottle of aftershave so tightly I'm surprised it doesn't shatter. I place it back carefully where I found it as he watches and raises a questioning eyebrow.

"I was snooping, sorry." I feel the blush that is bound to be staining my cheeks.

"Snoop away."

"I didn't get far, I got distracted by your aftershave actually." He picks it up and sprays a little on his neck with an overly confident grin and I genuinely worry that he can read my filthy mind. Either way, he looks like he'd like what he'd hear.

He holds a hand out for me. "Let's go, I want to take you somewhere."

CHAPTER THIRTEEN

Harriet

Instead of heading down to the seafront, this time we make our way along to Roker Park where Liam buys us both a Mr Whippy cone from the ice cream van complete with monkeys' blood (what we call raspberry sauce in the North East) and a 99 flake sticking out of the silky smooth ice cream.

The cast-iron bandstand in the middle of the park is where we sit, taking refuge from the intense heat of the sun. We're surrounded by vibrant blossom trees rustling in the breeze in time with the North Sea crashing in the distance. There's no one else around in this area of the park, not even a lone dog walker or a crowd of yummy mummies pushing prams, making it feel like our own private oasis.

"Tell me something about yourself," he says casually as we sit cross-legged, facing each other on the cool concrete.

"What do you want to know?" I'm not sure where to start with such an open-ended question.

"Let's start with something easy. Favourite musical?"

"*Six* is my all-time favourite because I was obsessed with Tudor history growing up and you know… girl power." I hold up my fist in solidarity with the six queens and give him a happy closed-eye smile. "What about you?"

"*Waitress*." His answer shouldn't surprise me, because like everything else about him, his answer is so completely unexpected I should have expected it.

"Is there a story there?" I ask, desperate to know more.

"Yeah, I've seen it live so many times, but my favourite performance has to be when Chelsea Halfpenny played Jenna. I mean, have you seen Chelsea perform 'She Used to Be Mine'?"

"I watched her perform on TV, but never in person."

"You need to, she's incredible."

"I thought you would have picked *Rock of Ages* or *Bat Out of Hell* or something after hearing the music coming from your dressing room this morning."

"I mean, I love rock and punk music, it's my go-to genre of music. But when it comes to musical theatre, *Waitress* has it all. The production is so prop heavy and is way more complex to call than ours so it's incredible to watch. Knowing what goes on behind the scenes with that many props and the sound and lighting cues in the show makes it even more entertaining for me I suppose. I have mad respect for everyone involved; it would be a dream come true to work on that production." His face lights up in a way I haven't seen before, at least, not when he's talking about his job. "My mam was a single mother and Jenna reminds me of her," he continues unprompted, referring to the main character. "Mam worked in a bakery and would always bring home sugary treats like pink slices and those old-school sponge cakes, you know, in the foil tray with the icing and sprinkles that you'd serve with Bird's custard." He smiles at the memory and I wonder how many times he gave her that smile when she came home. "She died when I was eighteen, bowel cancer took her too."

My heart aches for him, it's obviously tough to talk about. He averts his gaze, focusing on flicking some stones on the ground. I take his hand, squeezing it softly like he did to comfort me yesterday.

"Seems we have that in common then." I smiling tightly at him.

"Shitty, isn't it. It took her quickly, only three weeks, although the doctors said it was quite advanced. It's possible that she had it longer and didn't realise or she put the pain down to something else."

"Do you talk about her often?" I ask, wondering why he didn't mention it yesterday when I told him about Dad.

"Not as often as I should. Katie and her mam try to get me to talk about her, but it's tough, you know. Katie's mam is my mam's sister, they look so alike that on one hand it's comforting and on the other, it makes things really hard. I often wonder if this is what Mam would look like if she had had the chance to age, and then comes the guilt because Auntie Sarah took me in and supported me through my education," he says, revealing another softer sensitive side to him I'd not noticed.

"What about your dad?"

He bristles at the mention of him. "He wasn't around much. I didn't meet him until I was seven, even then I'd only see him at

Christmas and birthdays. He didn't want kids, I was the product of a one-night stand so I don't blame him, it's just... it would have been nice to have a dad growing up, instead he sent a monthly cheque with a note outlining what his expectations were of me that month. Sorry, I didn't mean to bring us both down. Tell me, what are your parents like?"

"I don't know what I'd do without them. They met in secondary school and have been married for over thirty years. Life has been really tough lately and honestly, I don't know how I would have coped without them."

"I bet they're really proud of you."

I ponder that for a moment.

"They say they are."

"You don't think it's true?" he seems genuinely confused at my response, so I continue.

"I can't get into the specifics because I signed an NDA, but I didn't exactly leave my last production on good terms. I'm not proud of it, so why would they be?" I shrug. "I don't mind. I just need to prove to everyone that I'm not a massive fuck-up anymore."

"Harriet, that doesn't mean they aren't proud of you. Who cares why you left, the fact you got there in the first place is a huge achievement. Not to mention I've been watching you this week and I'm already weirdly obsessed with your talent." He chuckles.

I reward him with a bashful smile, I've never had a problem taking a compliment, but from Liam, it hits differently and I'm not sure why.

"I don't know about you, but I really needed this talk

today," he says, taking the hint that I'm done talking for the day.

"Me too."

The peaceful atmosphere is interrupted by the alarm I set on my phone, reminding us that we have to make our way back to the theatre. Liam stands first and offers his hand to pull me up. We both look down to where our skin touches and I wonder if he feels the sense of comfort there too.

We choose to exit the park past the fairy dell and through Roker Ravine, a pathway carved out of the rock to create an entrance to the seafront.

Unlike our quiet paradise, the promenade is bustling with people enjoying the warm weather and calm sea. There are groups of kids playing football down on the sand, others making their way to the rocks with nets and buckets to see what they can find in the rock pools.

"I want to ask you something but don't know how to." Liam doesn't continue our walk so I turn to face him where he stands.

"You can ask me anything."

"My contract says I can't date anyone from the production." The words tumble from him as if he's been holding them in. "Does yours?"

"Yeah." I'm not sure how to react. I know Katie's doesn't mention relationships and other members of the cast are openly dating.

I also know exactly why mine has a relationship clause, but why his?

"I like you and if things were different, I would have asked you out the moment we met, but I can't. I wanted you to know anyway because I don't want you thinking I'm throwing you mixed signals by not asking you out when I'm obviously interested in you."

The air feels like it's been knocked out of me before I remember I need to speak.

"I like you too, like, way more than I probably should at this point, it's borderline pathetic." I add a humourless laugh, because it's Sod's law really, isn't it. I finally find someone I've really connected with and can't do anything about it.

"Thank god I'm not imagining it," he says, his lips in a resigned smile.

"It's kind of shitty, but it's probably a good thing. I've recently gotten out of what I thought was a committed relationship and promised myself I wouldn't rush into dating, especially with someone I work with. I already ruined my career once and by some miraculous twist of fate I got another chance. It'll never survive if it happens again," I try to explain without giving too much away.

"If you ever wanted to talk about it, I promise you can trust me," he says and I nod, knowing in my gut that's true, and that's completely terrifying.

CHAPTER FOURTEEN
Harriet

Liam isn't waiting for me this morning when I arrive at stage door. I'm a little sad if I'm completely honest but after yesterday's lunchtime confessions, it's probably for the best. At least, that's what I'm telling myself. I barely slept last night because now I know he feels the same way, it's all I can think about. I open the heavy door and turn to pull it closed behind me with both hands. When I turn around again, he's right there and I let out a little squeal, clutching my chest.

"Bloody hell! I almost had a heart attack!" I slap his arm in jest before erupting into uncontrollable giggling at the sight of him.

"Sorry, sorry," he says, panting, bending over with his hands on his knees, which only makes me laugh more. "I got… stuck on something… so I've… just sprinted. Phew."

He blows out a breath and straightens up, clutching his stomach with an over-dramatic grimace like he's got a stitch and we both collapse into laughter again.

"I didn't think you'd come this morning, after what we talked about yesterday…" I say trying to keep my voice low so we aren't overheard.

"I meant what I said, about this being my favourite part of the day."

My heart swells at his words.

"I meant it too."

We stand there grinning at each other like idiots for a few seconds before he breaks the silence.

"So, anyway. Good morning." God that smile with his perfect teeth and dimple in his cheek makes me weaker by the minute. This is not helping my already strained self-control.

No, I can't think like that. Be strong Harriet.

"Good morning," I reply as he holds open the green room door and follows me inside.

It's only been four days and he's already got me questioning my sanity. One minute I'm telling myself to back off, put some distance between us, and the next I'm thinking I should give in.

"No fact today?"

"Yeah, but you kept me waiting in suspense for you this morning, so I'm keeping you in suspense now..." I tease.

"Ah, a taste of my own medicine."

"Okay, you've suffered enough," I relent, and he barks out a laugh at how quickly I let him off the hook. "Did you know people say 'break a leg' before an audition because they hope you end up in a 'cast'?"

"Is that where it comes from?" He barks out a laugh in disbelief.

"Full disclosure, I saw it while scrolling on TikTok so it's probably a load of rubbish. It's a good joke though." I laugh. "What's on the agenda today in the wings," I ask as though I don't have access to his daily call sheet and have it memorised already.

"This morning we've been doing prep for the tech run tomorrow. There's also been a pretty significant change so you might want to get down to the stage as soon as possible," he says ominously.

"Tell me what you know," I say desperately, clutching his arm with both hands. I'm briefly distracted by his warm muscular forearm. He glances momentarily at where I'm holding him, and a knowing smile appears on his face.

"All I'm saying is that the rumours that have been circulating regarding a certain lead actress being delayed in London a little longer are true and that there are going to be significant casting changes." He gives me an extravagant wink, then steers me into my dressing room by my shoulders. "I'll see you soon."

"I'll see you down there," I say in excitement as he backs off, grinning, down the hallway.

Shortly after, Katie and I arrive at the stage and we begin stretching, preparing for the day ahead. People are already whispering to each other; the rumour mill is operating at full capacity today.

"Can I have everyone's attention please," Robert says, standing in the middle of the stage so we can all see him. "I have some news... As you may notice, Rachael is not here because she has been delayed by her work commitments for TV, so, Harriet, we need you to swing in for the lead for the foreseeable. We're putting on costumes today so we can take some promo pics, so let's get to it."

As much as Liam had prepared me for this, I'm stunned. I'm immediately pulled into a hug by Zach with Katie throwing her arms around both of us with an excited squeal.

"You're going to be amazing!" Zach says as the rest of the cast join us to celebrate.

When we pull apart my eyes immediately search for Liam. He mouths congratulations to me from the other side of the stage and I wish I could talk to him and debrief this moment, but there's no time. As soon as the meeting is over, our dance captain is already calling us to start for the day.

We stretch some more and run through some breathing exercises, which really help to centre my now chaotic thoughts, not only is my mind on Liam but now performing the lead part to a home crowd on opening night has my stomach in nervous excited knots.

It's a big deal and an opportunity I can't mess up.

If this isn't a sign that I need to focus, I don't know what is. I'm just going to have to be stern with myself, I can totally push away those thoughts about Liam and make this a killer performance.

"Are you as hyped up as I am right now?" A voice in the doorway of my dressing room says a little while later. Zach comes in and makes himself comfortable in Katie's chair.

"I know, I don't quite believe it," I say, still on my high. "There are a few things we've not gone over yet though, so I guess we need to do some more rehearsal and I suppose we should talk about the intimate scenes too?"

"That's a good idea," he agrees.

"This one specifically," I say, handing him the script at an open page. "There's a lot of physical movement for us to choreograph for this scene, and I was hoping we could discuss the actual kiss."

"I have no preference to whether we kiss or fake it; I've done plenty of stage kisses over the years and it doesn't bother me. As long as you're comfortable, I'm good. And whatever choice you make I'll back you up one hundred per cent."

"Thank you," I say, appreciative of his thoughtfulness. "I'm happy to keep it real. This scene is so emotionally charged, it'll probably come across more genuine if it was a real kiss. If that's good for you?"

"I totally agree with you there. I'm happy to practice if you want to get the first one out of the way? Oh god, sorry that sounded like a line. I wasn't..." His cheeks are so purple with embarrassment he resembles a beetroot, and I let out a chuckle.

"Zach, relax, I knew what you meant, but thank you for being so considerate of my feelings." I squeeze his shoulder lightly.

"Always, and if you change your mind or don't feel comfortable at any point, please tell me," he says, and I'm glad I'm doing this with someone who has quickly become a close friend.

"Zach, Harriet, we're ready in wardrobe," Robert says, making a rare dressing room visit. "We really want to push the marketing this week. You're local talent so we want to plaster your faces everywhere. I've got marketing coming in tonight to discuss your own social media too."

A loud ringing fills the room coming from Robert's pocket so he pauses the conversation to answer the call.

"What do you mean the photographer is unavailable? … Are you serious? … We need the photos today! … Fine I'll figure something out, give me five." He hangs up and places his phone in his pocket. "Sorry, our photographer has dropped out, hang out here for now while I try to find a new one."

"My sister is an event photographer. She's done work for the Sunderland Empire and Wearside FC. It's her day off today, but I could call in a favour."

"You're saving this production in more ways than you know, Harriet Adams, I won't forget this!" Robert says, leaving the room as quickly as he arrived.

CHAPTER FIFTEEN
Liam

The radio on my hip begins to crackle, the tell-tale sign Di is about to issue a task.

"Liam, can you go to stage door to collect Jayne Adams," Di's voice comes through the speaker. "Bring her to the auditorium, she's the new photographer."

"Copy that," I reply and make my way to collect Harriet's sister.

Other than the length and colour of her hair, she looks exactly like Harriet. She's dressed in a black tank top and skinny jeans and has a large camera bag over her shoulder as well as the two large duffle bags resting at her feet.

I introduce myself and pick up the bags so I can escort her through the maze that is backstage.

"So, you're the boy that has my big sister in such a tizzy, huh?" she says as we walk. "Do I need to give you the 'If you break her heart, I will murder you in your sleep' speech? Because believe me, I'd do time for her. The last guy she was with did a number on her and I'll be damned if I let that happen again."

"I think that covers it." I laugh nervously, because I don't doubt that she or Harriet would do time to protect the other. She narrows her eyes at me when I stop in the corridor and look around to make sure I'm not overheard. "I want to talk to you about something, I was wondering if I could come around and talk to your dad tomorrow? Harriet is playing the lead on opening night and I want to invite him to watch the show. It might not be possible for him, he'll have to see how he feels at the time, but if I got the measurements of his chair in advance, I'd need half an hour before the doors open to take out some seats to give him enough space. I know it would mean a lot to her."

"You'd do that? Wow." She seems genuinely taken back by my suggestion. "I thought you only wanted to get in her pants or something, but you actually care, don't you?"

"Yeah, we're friends."

"Okay," she scoffs. "Give me your number and I'll text you when he's up tomorrow."

"Thanks." I type in my number and pass back her phone. "Can we keep this between us for now? I don't want to get Harriet's hopes up in case my plan doesn't work out."

"Sure, your secret is safe with me." She mimes zipping her mouth, locking it and throwing away the key with a smile.

I wish I could go back in time, I really fucking do, because I chose the worst possible moment to walk into the wings.

Harriet and Zach are rehearsing, which is totally fine, I mean, it's their job. But they're rehearsing a scene in which Harriet's character has a scorching-hot sex dream scene where

Zach's character goes down on her and honestly, my jealousy takes me completely by surprise. Obviously, I already knew the script, I knew what I'd have to watch from my work area in the shadows but that was before I'd met her and before I'd even contemplated what it might actually look like.

What I didn't consider is the fact that one of my closest friends would be kissing her before I had the chance to, and it feels like a punch to the gut.

"Now you're the one that looks about ready to murder someone in their sleep," Jayne's voice comes from behind me with a laugh.

"Oh, fuck!" I jump a foot in the air at her unexpected arrival. I hadn't realised I had been so tense until the sudden shock loosened me up. I look at my palms that have crescent indents from where I had balled my fists.

"You know that's fake, yeah?" The way she teases me reminds me of Katie and I instantly feel a younger sisterly connection to her.

Just as quick as the scene started, it's over and my heart finally stops pounding in my ears.

"Yeah, I know it's fake. Obviously. I've read the script." I roll my eyes.

"So why are your hands in fists and your voice an octave higher than it was ten minutes ago?"

"I don't know what you're talking about." I try to make my voice deeper but it comes out far too deep this time and Jayne gives me the side eye like I've lost my mind. She is not wrong.

"Jesus Christ, I thought she was the one who's gone full 'Boyle,' now I think it might be you."

"What?" I ask, confused.

"Ha! That reference is spot on!" Katie says, coming to stand on my other side. "You'll have to excuse my cousin, he's one of those weirdos that haven't watched each season of *Brooklyn Nine-Nine* at least five times."

I stop listening to the girls as they bond around me over a TV show, instead, I focus on Harriet.

"Guys, that was amazing," the intimacy director says. "Next there's a strobe lighting effect which will distract the audience so Zach can jump down off the bed and Harriet can wake up from her dream with a gasp. Shall we start again and add in the effects now that VFX are here?" She looks to Robert who nods. "Great, let's go again."

Robert directs the scene to begin again and I groan, turning away, pained with yet more jealousy at the sight of Zach's position between Harriet's legs.

Jayne snickers. "Act cool, man."

"He can't, he's programmed to overthink everything," Katie chips in.

"Shut up," I hiss at her, my jaw tense.

"This must be killing you, huh. It's so hot, they have great on-stage chemistry," Katie adds, and I glare at her.

"He looks marginally less murderous than he did the first time he watched them so I'd say it's an improvement," Jayne says, looking around me to Katie again. "I'm Jayne. Harriet's sister.

Thought I better introduce myself since Liam wasn't going to."

"God, Liam, you're so rude. I'm Katie." She holds her hand out to shake Jayne's.

I look between the mischievous pair and shake my head. No matter what I say I'll be digging myself a hole, so I go with the safe option and say nothing.

"What are you going to do about it then?" Jayne asks me, just like Zach and Katie did the other night.

"What do you mean, what am I going to do about it?" I try to buy time, because I've no idea how to navigate this.

"She literally could not be clearer," Katie says, earning herself another glare from me, which doesn't faze her one bit.

"Okay, this," I point between my meddlesome little cousin and Harriet's little sister, "fucking scares me."

"I'm serious, what are you going to do about it?" Katie asks again.

"We've agreed to ignore our feelings and co-exist as friends and colleagues."

"Okay," they both scoff, and honestly, I'm getting bored of that reaction. "When you want advice on how to woo my sister, you know where I am," Jayne adds.

Jayne is called to the stage and leaves us with a friendly nod. I breathe an audible sigh of relief that the interrogation is over.

"I like her, she's cool," Katie says matter-of-factly and walks off in the opposite direction.

I'm thankful the rehearsal of that scene is over; I've got a two-hour reprieve as I assist Jayne with the photo shoot and then they just have to rehearse the other kissing scenes. They're less of a 'rip-each-other's-clothes-off' kind of kiss so, I mean, it can't be worse than watching Zach pretend to go down on her.

Right?

Wrong, I was very, very wrong.

One whole hour.

That's how long I watch Harriet kiss Zach as if he's the love of her life. No tongues obviously, but their kiss was tender and loving and electric. They're fantastic actors, and if I didn't know better, I'd swear their romance was real.

From a production point of view, it's going to be great; the audience is going to lap it up and really buy into the romance between the characters but, fuck, this is not good for my self-esteem.

CHAPTER SIXTEEN
Harriet

"Is it always this full on?" Jayne asks me when we pile into the car that evening after a hectic day.

"Yeah, they don't call it 'Hell Week' for nothing."

"I've never heard you call it that?"

"I don't like the phrase, yeah it's hard work and exhausting but it's my dream and there are plenty of actors out there that would kill for this."

She turns out of the car park onto Whitburn Road that hugs the Seaburn coast and I rest my head on the headrest, looking out of the passenger window towards the sea. The sun set about an hour ago, but the sky is still a dusky pink, blending into purple and deep blue at the horizon.

My phone vibrates with the call sheet for tomorrow and as expected it's another busy day.

"Speaking of full on, I just got my call sheet for tomorrow. Want to hear?" She nods. "9:30 full company rehearsal on stage. 10:45 get ready for tech rehearsal one, which starts at 11:15. Lunch at 12:30, back into costume at 1:30 for tech rehearsal two at 2 p.m, 5:45 dinner, 6:45 back into costume for 7 p.m. dress rehearsal and then end of calls at 10 p.m."

"I'm exhausted thinking about it." She sighs dramatically.

"Yeah, but it's a good kind of exhausted. It'll be worth it when we see the finished product."

"I really enjoyed watching you today. Although, seeing you pretend to have sex on stage was a little weird," she adds with a grimace, and I laugh. "Katie, Zach and Liam are cool, I can see why you're friends with them."

"Yeah, for the most part everyone is cool, but they're the best."

It's not long before we're pulling onto the driveway. Dad's bedroom light is on, so I assume he's still awake, which is nice, the long days have meant I haven't seen him much this week.

I pop my head in the door and am rewarded by a wonderful smile. He's sitting with his reading glasses on flicking through a copy of the latest *National Geographic* magazine.

"You look a bit perkier, Dad." I take a seat next to him.

"They've got me on these new pain drugs and they're great, less sleepy side effects than the others," he says with an enthusiastic smile.

"I'm glad!" I smile.

"Tell me, how was it?" He pats the side of his bed.

Of course, I had sent him a message earlier in the day to tell him the news, but as I relay the events of the day to him another wave of excitement comes over me.

Despite everything I went through in London, despite losing it all, I finally feel like I'm taking back control of my life.

My arrival at stage door is a lonely one this morning. Liam isn't coming in until later today.

I don't think I realised just how much I need that five minutes of alone time we've had together each morning this week.

Now that I know that my attraction isn't one sided it makes it much harder to stay away from him, although, the fact that we could both lose our jobs is a good enough reason to live with the torture of not being able to have him.

A prime example of me not being able to stay away is loading up his Instagram so I can send him a voice note.

"Good morning. Today's fun fact is brought to you all the way from Broadway! The filmed version of Hamilton was recorded scene by scene from various angles over three days, not as one whole performance. That's all. I hope you have a nice morning and I'll see you later."

My phone dings almost immediately with a reply.

"Good morning. I thought I was going to miss my fact today. I wish I could have seen you this morning, but the voice message makes it a little better."

Shit, he sounds tired and sexy and was that a bed spring I could hear in the background? I get all hot and flustered thinking about him in bed, his eyes all sleepy and his hair a mess. The reaction that image has on my body is strictly NSFW. Much like the dream I had last night of the two of us. Thinking about it has me wafting cool air over my face.

I open the door to my dressing room and am relieved Katie

isn't here yet. I pull the loose messy bun from my hair so it cascades down my back and quickly tear off my baggy hoodie to reveal my leotard and tracksuit bottoms. Before my sensible mind can make me see sense, I open the camera on my phone. I've never been great at taking selfies so instead I rearrange my boobs in my Lycra top to show maximum cleavage and carefully position myself to take a mirror selfie.

Do I bend seductively towards the mirror and arch my back to make my boobs look perkier?

Yes, yes, I do.

After all, he said he wished he could see me – this is the next best thing.

"Does this make up for it?"

I attach the photo and send the voice message before I can think better of it. I know I'm playing with fire here because without looking at that picture again I'm ninety-nine per cent sure you can see my nipples peeking out through my thin leotard, a by-product of me thinking dirty thoughts about him.

"Fucking hell, you look incredible. My self-control is barely hanging on by a thread as it is, now I'm ready to say fuck it let's put ourselves out of this misery."

I lay back on the chaise longue, and an uncontrollable grin reaches from ear to ear when I listen to his message. I'm back to being all hot and bothered by the sound of his voice.

A second later a picture pops onto my screen and the moment I see it I want to commit it to my eternal memory. Liam is shirtless with crisp white bedding gathered around his waist. His dark brown hair is all mussed and his eyes are still glassy from sleep. He's everything I imagined he'd be on a morning and I want nothing more than to burrow into his arms and stay there forever.

But we can't go there, can we?

I sit up again, putting my phone face down and take a deep breath, already feeling the overwhelming sense of anxiety wash over me. This is wrong, we both have so much to lose here. I pick my phone up again and type a message to tell him this is wrong but delete it and start again a dozen times, unable to find the words without coming across as unhinged.

How can I tell him this is wrong? It doesn't feel wrong at all, in fact, it feels natural, as if we've been friends for years instead of a week.

A few minutes of silent panicking pass, and after many attempts to draft a message to keep him at arm's length, my phone rings and even though I don't have the number saved, I know it's him so I answer right away.

"Liam," I barely recognise my voice; it comes out uneven and breathless as if I'm on the edge of a breakdown.

"Katie gave me your number yesterday. I hope you don't mind me calling. I keep seeing those little text bubbles pop up and then they stop and start again. Are you freaking out?"

"Yeah, a little."

"Harriet, I'm sorry. I didn't mean to come on too strong," he says, apologising for something that isn't his fault. I'm the one who started it with that indecent nipple pic.

"It's not that, I liked the picture, a lot. I liked it so much my teeth hurt." The words tumble out of me in a nonsensical jumble.

"Your teeth hurt?" His worry quickly turns to amusement, but he doesn't laugh at me, and I appreciate that.

"Yeah, I can't explain it. I feel like... seeing you like that... when I want... ugh! You make my teeth hurt!" I'm rambling now, and I still don't think I'm making any sense at all, but I can't help it. "And apparently you turn me into an idiot too."

"Hey, calm down. I understand perfectly, you make my teeth hurt too." His voice is so reassuring it doesn't seem that stupid when he says it. I can hear him smile and it puts me at ease. "This situation is tough, we like each other, clearly. But we can't act on it and that's shit."

"We need to be careful, Liam. Our careers are on the line here. I won't be the reason you lose your job."

"Harriet—"

"It's not only that, I meant what I said about protecting my own career. I don't want to get a reputation for shagging people I work with." I groan when a call comes over the speakers telling me I have ten minutes to get to the stage to start the day. "I should go."

"It's going to be okay Harriet."

I don't know how he can be so sure but I trust the calming conviction in his words.

When the dressing room door opens and shuts, Katie is the one who interrupts us this time. She walks into the dressing room, discarding her jacket and bag and looks at me quizzically when she notices I'm on the phone. I mouth the word 'Liam' which only makes her bounce her eyebrows at me and do some sort of pelvic hip thrust, so I roll my eyes and turn away.

"I've got to go, Katie's arrived and I think she's having some sort of seizure," I say, explaining my sudden distraction.

"Har-har, you're soooo funny!" she says loud enough for Liam to hear, her voice dripping with sarcasm.

"I'll see you after lunch," I say, turning my attention back to the phone.

"Have a good morning, and please don't overthink anything until I get there so we can overthink together."

"I'll try." I hang up and put my phone out of sight before I do something stupid like send him another photo.

CHAPTER SEVENTEEN
Harriet

Social media has never been my strong point, so Oscar the TikTok and Instagram mastermind has agreed to help me with my accounts in a bid to increase interest in the show. He wants me to go viral and I have no idea how to do that. I'm fine with posting photos and posting to my stories but apparently, there's a science behind hashtags and reels and when Oscar tells me about them, he might as well be speaking a foreign language.

So far, my posts and stories have been enough for my ten thousand followers but, compared to Oscar's content, the engagement on my page is clearly lacking.

"Okay, why do these people follow you?" he asks me, pacing the floor of the green room impatiently when I've failed to grasp the question of 'who is your target market?' for the third time.

"Because I'm a performer." By no means am I a celebrity, but within musical theatre, I'm well known among the fandoms, especially since my last show had a huge cult following.

"Okay, so this stuff that you've been posting is great because people are nosy AF, but what they also want are sneak peaks of your performances and BTS content."

"The South Korean boyband?"

He rolls his eyes at me. "OMG," he spells the letters out, laughing. "I am so surprised at your K-Pop knowledge."

"Oh, I have no knowledge, I see people posting about them all the time."

"What I mean is 'behind the scenes'. You've got a killer set of lungs, babe, the humans in your phone want to hear you sing," he says flamboyantly.

"But we can't record the show," Katie chips in from her spot on the sofa.

"No, but you can record TikTok videos in your costume around the theatre. You can record a day in the life, you can record yourself having fun, Q and As or even messing around in the dressing room. I've heard you both freestyling in here, record stuff like that and you'll be viral in no time," he says, ticking the options off on his fingers.

"I like those ideas!" I say, writing the suggestions down. "And the lead up to opening night tomorrow will be perfect for a day in the life!"

This evening, when Katie invites me out for drinks I agree and drag along Jayne too. She turned up at the theatre after spending part of her day shooting portraits in her studio saying she had free time and wanted to take more photographs here and edit the ones she took yesterday.

She likes being in the theatre, it's a nice distraction for her.

The dress rehearsal earlier this evening ran perfectly. Zach and I nailed the production and the entire company wanted to celebrate, albeit a quiet celebration since we've all spent over thirteen hours working today and have another long day tomorrow.

We fill two full tables upstairs at The Stack, on one side, there are the twinkling lights of the ships out to sea and on the other, the live band is playing.

A welcome breeze whips around us and that first sip of gin cools me.

Me, Liam, Jayne, Katie, Zach and Oscar sit at one table and I honestly can't remember the last time I smiled and laughed so much. For the first time in a long time, surrounded by my sister and my friends, I feel happy.

"If I can have everyone's attention," Robert says, standing between our tables a little while later, we've all stopped drinking now since a hangover in the morning would not be ideal but none of us seem ready to go home yet. "I would just like to say a big heartfelt thank you to everyone. This week has been tough, especially with the short notice casting changes, but you've each handled the challenge with grace and professionalism. Here's to us and our production. We'll be at the Olivier awards before you know it! Cheers!" he concludes, holding up his glass of lemonade, and we all echo him as he takes his seat next to Di again before continuing our individual conversations.

"I need the loo," Katie says meaningfully, meeting my eye.

"Oh, yes. Me too," I say, getting the hint and following her towards the ladies room.

"So, Jayne. What's her deal?" Katie asks when we're alone

in the toilets, neither of us bothering to go into a stall.

"What's her deal?" I ask.

"Yeah, like who is more her type, Zach or me?"

"I mean, you and Zach are like complete opposites. He's sunshine wrapped up in a nice clean parcel and you're definitely more of a grump."

"I mean gender wise; I'm definitely getting a vibe, but I don't know if that's wishful thinking on my part," she says, uncharacteristically unsure of herself.

"She's never officially come out, but I know she's dated women and men before."

"Okay, so would you be okay if I asked her out?" she asks, twisting her hands together nervously; it's kind of adorable.

"Of course, but remember this," I say, pointing my forefinger at her, trying my best to appear threatening. "You break her heart, I'll murder you in your sleep."

"Funny, she said the exact same thing to Liam the other day, but she looked a lot more menacing than you," she says with a hint of a smile.

"Yeah, we get that a lot." I shrug.

"Okay, glad we got this cleared up. Let's get out there so I can put the moves on your sister," she says, pumping herself up.

"Oh, great. Just what a sister wants to see," I say in jest, if it makes Jayne happy, that's all that matters to me.

"I don't want to watch you eye-fucking my cousin, but here we are." She glances at me meaningfully.

"I have not been doing that," I say as we wind our way back

through the tables.

"Look me in the eye and tell me you're not imagining him naked when you look at him." She's got me there because I can't stop picturing him in bed since he sent that photo this morning. In my imagination I'm right there with him.

"I'm not…" She stops to turn to me, scoffing in disbelief. "Okay, fine. I am. But keep it to yourself."

I turn her back around and nudge her forward again. Katie has a spring in her step on our way back to the table. She jumps into my seat next to Jayne where the two of them exchange shy glances and it's quite cute to watch Katie a little nervous. Since Katie is now in my seat, that leaves her seat next to Liam free for me and I send her a silent thank you too. As I sit, Liam shifts and leans slightly closer to me, propping himself up with his hand on the bench right behind me. If you weren't paying attention, you'd have missed it, but I for one, am paying rapt attention.

I haven't spoken more than two words to Liam that didn't involve the show since he came back to work this afternoon. The dress rehearsal is like a normal show, so we were both flat out busy until the performance was over. Afterwards, I went straight to hair and wardrobe to drop off my wig and costume and came here with Katie and Zach while he was putting the set and props back together for opening night tomorrow.

There's still so much left unsaid between us and a busy bar surrounded by our colleagues isn't the place to have the conversation. So, we make small talk with our friends as Diane watches us like a hawk from the other end of the room.

Eventually, the crowd thins out until there are a few of us left at our table. With Diane having left for the evening, Liam and I are sitting so close our thighs are pressed together and although there is plenty of space for us to spread out, neither of us move an inch. The chemistry I've been trying to ignore all night is screaming in my ears as everyone around us disappears when he leans down to speak quietly in my ear.

"You look so beautiful tonight."

A shiver runs down my spine as my body involuntarily leans towards him. Incoherent thoughts about this being wrong flit through my mind, but I ignore them. I've said this many times over the past few days but there is no way this is wrong when it feels so right.

When I look up into his hazel eyes, I can hear his thoughts in my mind as though he's speaking aloud. His emotions are clear on his face and in the heavy rise and fall of his chest.

I want you. I hear him think.

Take me, please, I'm yours.

My internal voice is not above begging.

When someone clears their throat loudly, we snap out of our trance and I become all too aware of how close we are, our faces barely inches apart. We're so close that if I just move a little more, I could end this torture and kiss him right there in front of everyone.

I could, but I shouldn't.

"I think I'm ready to go home," I say, standing quickly, almost falling over the back of the bench, my voice much louder than necessary.

"Yeah, me too." Jayne also stands abruptly, sensing my impending panic. I'm so thankful to have her right now.

I quickly wave goodbye to the others and turn to leave the bar without a second glance at Liam.

I was far too close to giving in that time and he was too.

CHAPTER EIGHTEEN
Liam

I haven't seen Harriet in person since she left the bar so abruptly last night. I don't know if it was the burst of chemistry between us that scared her off or my eagerness. It felt like the world was going to end if I didn't do something. I honestly don't know if I should be thanking Zach for his obvious coughing that broke us from the dream-like moment or wringing his neck for cock-blocking me.

If it were just me at risk, there would be no question about it, I would have kissed her.

As if my thoughts summon her, she appears in the doorway, looking like a dream, with her hair in tight pin curls and a wig cap. Her make-up is done and she wears a mic belt around her waist ready for me to fit her mic.

"Hey, do you mind if I go live on Instagram for this? I want to demonstrate to people how we prepare for mic fittings and things," she asks as she walks into the dressing room reserved for the hair department, holding up her phone attached to a small tripod, and I nod in agreement.

She's been doing a day in the life feature on Instagram and Facebook today to promote the show and as far as I can tell people are loving it. I've been watching the updates on her stories all morning, obsessing over every little detail in the Q & A, drinking in every little fact I learn about her.

She takes her seat, offering me a giddy smile that I return. It's only because of the post she recorded in warm-up and posted five minutes ago that I was prepared for her to walk in here wearing nothing but a flimsy sports bra with spaghetti straps and grey jogging bottoms rolled down at the waist showing off her smooth stomach.

"Shall we do this then?" I ask, and she nods enthusiastically. She leans forward, pressing the screen, setting the video to 'live,' meeting my eye and giving me a shy smile in the mirror.

"I'm waiting for more people to start watching," she explains, and I rest my hands on her bare shoulders so I can lean over her to look at the small screen, my mouth close to her ear.

"What are those numbers in the top corner?" Goosebumps appear on her neck as I speak. My satisfied smile is mirrored back to me from her phone, I know exactly what the numbers are, I just needed an excuse to get close to her.

"That's how many people are watching us right now," she says, turning to look at me so there's only inches between us. I watch her through the phone as her eyes linger on my mouth for a few seconds longer than is probably appropriate.

"Are you going to tell those lovely people watching us what we're going to be doing today?" I ask, turning to look at her. Her eyes widen as she glances from me to the phone as if she forgot it was recording.

"Oh, right... Yeah... Hey, everyone!" she says, the number of viewers steadily rising into the high hundreds. I keep my hands firmly planted on her shoulders and wonder if her heart is pounding as hard as mine. "I'm in the hair department about to have my wig fitted, which is why I have this attractive wig cap on my head. But, before I do that, I need my microphone fitted. The gorgeous Liam here is one of our assistant stage managers and he is helping me out with my mic today. If you have any questions for either me or Liam, post them in the comments and we'll try and answer as many as we can."

She leans forward slightly to read some of the comments that are coming in.

"Oh, please keep the comments PG," she says blushing, so I lean over her shoulder one again to read them and immediately blush. "Looks like you've got yourself some fans here, Liam," she adds with a chuckle.

"I am flattered, thank you," I say as I read the comments, trying to find some that are more appropriate for me to answer. "Uh, I've worked for this production company for eight years now. I do a lot of different things. There's myself and another ASM, a deputy stage manager and a stage manager who oversees everything you see happening on stage. We deal with props, wardrobe, the movements of the set, we keep the cast in check..." I knead Harriet's shoulders and she laughs.

"It's true, he does," she agrees, nodding.

"My official title is ASM, but I would say I'm more of a

technical swing as I tend to swing in and out of different departments as and when I'm needed, so my day to day is never the same."

I laugh when I see the next question. "Am I single?" I say thoughtfully. "Hmm, I am, but I wish I wasn't."

As I stand up straighter, I brush my hands down Harriet's arms and I see her smile reflected in the mirror as she looks at me.

"Okay, that's enough of those kinds of questions. If you have any questions relating to Liam's job then type away," she says with a nervous laugh, breaking our eye contact and addressing the camera again. "Let's get started."

"Okay. This is Harriet's microphone for today," I say, holding up the mic, placing my hand behind it to focus the camera. "It's called a head mic. It fits over her ears and the boom part fits snugly against her cheek. There are several types of microphones productions use such as single over ear mics and hairline mics, but we use these. The main reason is because our show has a band on stage, which means it can get very loud, by using these we have a lot more control over the sounds that are picked up."

Harriet smiles at me when I meet her eye in the mirror again.

"Sorry, did I get too technical?"

"No, not at all, that was great, please continue."

"Usually, we match the mic to the colour of the actor's hair but since our lovely Harriet is a natural brunette and her wig is blonde, we match it to the wig so you'll see that the wires and the mic itself are a sandy colour to match not only the hair colour but also her skin tone."

I concentrate as I place the mic over her ears and secure in place, noticing her breath catch ever so slightly and the tiny little raised bumps that appear on her skin where I've brushed her.

"I'm using a little bit of this mic tape to secure it here just next to her ear, which will keep the microphone in place. The tape will be covered by the wig in Harriet's case but if you ever see a little bit of tape on a performer's face it'll be this stuff. It's a little like surgical tape so it doesn't irritate the skin and can be removed easily and painlessly after the performance."

I study my work to make sure everything is where it's meant to be, turning her to the side and tilting her face gently with my fingertips, giving the camera a full view of what I'm doing.

"You're such a perfectionist," she teases as I adjust the mic barely a millimetre.

"Only when it comes to you." A blush stains her cheeks, and her eyes widen in surprise. Probably because I'm openly flirting with her on camera, but luckily there's nothing in either of our contracts about flirting.

"When it comes to the remainder of the wire," I say, addressing the camera again. "The mic pack is going to be held in this belt around her waist underneath her costume. Harriet, can you stand and turn to the side please?" She does as I ask, but in our current position, I'm blocking the camera, so placing my hands on the soft, warm skin of her hips, I turn her ever so slightly.

"Is this a better position?" she asks innocently, but the mischief in her eyes and the smirk she gives me tells me she means so much more.

"Much," I say, clearing my throat.

She bends her neck so I can twist and secure the wire with more tape while I give a half-arsed reason why I do this because all the blood has left my brain and settled down south. I smooth the wire down the length of her spine and my hands visibly tremble as I tape the wire in place.

For the entire time I'm touching her, I have to fight with myself not to do something stupid that will get us sacked live on Instagram. She looks over her shoulder at me and when our eyes linger, I can see a similar war going on behind hers.

"Perfect," I say in a whisper before clearing my throat and looking away.

We return to our original position, her sitting facing the camera and me standing behind her, holding onto her shoulders, anchoring myself to her.

"I'll scroll through some of these comments and questions." Her voice is shaky, and I wonder if she's as turned on as I am. All that touching and stroking down her back has turned me into a horny teenager unable to control my body's reactions.

"Oh," she says, the blush returning to her cheeks, only this time instead of a light pinkish colour, she's fire engine red, so I lean over her shoulder to read again.

You have got to be fucking, if not you need to be because that was the most erotic thing I've ever seen.

That was hotter than porn and neither of you took your clothes off followed by an emoji of a drooling face and a red face with its tongue hanging out.

Hundreds of comments echo their same thoughts.

"I can't read most of these comments out." She laughs, covering her mouth in disbelief.

"On that note, I think it's time for us to sign off," I say.

We say our goodbyes and switch off the camera. She takes her phone from the tripod and makes sure the video posts to her Instagram before putting it down again.

"That was crazy," I say. "Over three thousand people watched me fit your microphone."

"For some reason, I don't think they we're concentrating on the mic fitting, more so our little show. You were very popular."

"Are you jealous?" I ask, sitting in the seat next to her. I turn it to face her and scooch closer. She looks around, checking no one can overhear us, before facing me. We're so close my thighs encase hers.

"I was a little bit jealous, I'll admit," she says, her cheeks pink again.

"I'm all yours if you want me," my voice is a whisper now, openly admitting how close I am to giving in. "All you have to do is say the word, Harriet, and I'll give myself to you in a heartbeat."

"You know we can't, Liam." Her words are laced with regret.

"I know," I say, taking her hand and looking down as she weaves her fingers through mine.

I'm about to speak again when my radio announces that I'm needed in the wings.

"You should go," she says, her voice low, but before I do, I place one soft kiss on her cheek.

CHAPTER NINETEEN
Harriet

Ever since I was little, I've had pre-show jitters and today is no different, the added pressure of playing the lead to a home crowd has my nerves sky high.

"Harriet?" Liam says from the open door of my dressing room where Katie and I are patiently waiting for our places call. "Would you come with me for just a minute please?"

"Yeah sure, what's up?" I ask, glancing to Katie for a hint.

"You'll see," he says with a flick of his head, encouraging me to follow him.

When we're far enough from the populated areas of backstage, Liam takes my hand, entwining our fingers, and leads me through the unused corridors and up to the top floor of the building. I know I shouldn't, but I let him keep my hand in his, enjoying how it feels.

We pause at the door that leads to a private room in the auditorium on the gallery level. There are two private viewing boxes in towers on either side of the stage.

The boxes aren't in use anymore as they have less than a fifteen per cent view of the stage, pointless really, but desirable when the theatre was first built. This was where the upper-class people of Sunderland would come. The rich families that owned shipyards and coal mines, or even the Whitton Family themselves would have spent the evening here. The purpose of this area was not to watch but to be seen instead, flaunting their wealth to the working-class people who were only able to afford unreserved gallery seats.

When we push through the door and step down into the box, voices drift through the large open space. I can hear the murmurings and excitement of the crowd as people file into the auditorium. There's nothing quite like the atmosphere of an excited audience; I can already feel the buzz running through my veins.

Liam had the foresight to turn the light off in the little room so as not to draw attention to us, after all, I'm in costume and the gallery is already filling up. He puts the torch on his phone to illuminate the floor so we can see where we're stepping as we cross to the balcony, looking out.

No one so much as glances our way.

"Look down there, at the stalls," he says, only now letting go of my hand, and I lean forward to peer over the edge.

"Is that my dad?" I gasp, but I already know the answer. Liam nods and passes me a tissue, noticing my eyes have filled with tears.

"I didn't want to tell you until I knew for certain he would make it. But he was really determined to come tonight."

"You've spoken to him?"

"That's why I was late yesterday, I went to your house to

meet him and ask him to come tonight. I hope I didn't overstep," he says, doubt flashing in his eyes.

A lump forms in my throat as I struggle to compose myself. I can't answer him with words, so I push him deep into the shadows and throw my arms around his neck, pulling him closer and refusing to let go.

I take a deep inhale, wanting to remember everything about this moment from the feel of his body pressed against mine to the scent of his aftershave. Liam does the same, his face pressed to my neck as he takes a deep breath in too, releasing it with a sigh as I massage the nape of his neck with my fingers.

"Thank you," I whisper, and lean back slightly so I can dab at the tears still threatening to ruin my make-up.

Liam keeps an arm wrapped around my waist, as though he's not ready to let me go yet, and I'm thankful, because I don't want him to. He places his palm against my cheek, caressing me, comforting and soothing me.

"Thank you," I say again. "From the bottom of my heart, you have no idea what this means to us."

"I'd do anything to make you happy, Harriet. I truly mean it." It's moments like this I wish I could kiss him, so I turn my face to the hand holding my face and kiss the inside of his wrist softly.

Words don't seem enough to express how grateful I am in this moment. My dad will be watching me from the front row of the audience tonight because of this man right here. This man who hasn't known me long but has already made such an enormous impact on my life. I'm closer to Liam than I ever was to any of my so-called 'friends' in London, even the man I was in a relationship with knew less about my family life than I've shared with Liam. He knew how important it was for my dad to see me perform potentially for the last time and made it happen against all odds because he wanted to see me happy.

"I don't deserve you," I say, my voice uneven, tears still threatening to spill.

"You deserve this, Harriet, your dad is so proud of you and now he'll get to see you perform in a place that's important to both of you," he says.

I hook my hand behind his neck and pull him closer, resting my forehead against his and running my hand over his jaw. He lets out a breath, an even mixture of contentment and frustration.

My eyes drop to his mouth, wanting nothing more than to just be with him, and I whisper, "All we have to do is get through the next few months and then we can renegotiate our contracts."

He nods in understanding. We can wait a few months, right?

We stay like this, holding each other in the darkness for a few moments until a crackle comes over the radio attached to Liam's hip with our places call.

"We better go," he says, running his hands down my arms and entwining his fingers with mine.

"You go first, I want to take this in for a second longer."

He kisses me on the cheek, then backs away but doesn't let go of my hands until our arms no longer reach. The embrace is nowhere near enough but it's all I'm allowed at the moment, and

I'll take all I can get.

At the end of the show, we do our usual curtain call and Dad is there in the front row beaming up at me. I can see that he's tired, but his eyes are brighter than I've seen them for a long time.

The entire audience are on their feet cheering and clapping. This is like nothing I've ever heard; the sheer volume of the crowd's appreciation is overwhelming. The cast bow to the audience, then the band and finally, the director. Robert catches my eye and flicks his head towards Dad, giving me permission to head out into the audience. I run down the stairs at the side of the stage as quickly as my feet will carry me. I carefully wrap my arms around my dad, snuggling into his frail chest, and he kisses my head softly as my mam and Jayne both join our hug.

I don't think there's a dry eye in the house following our embrace. I can even hear people sobbing above the booming applause, or maybe it's coming from me and my family, I'm not exactly paying attention.

"I'm so proud of you," Dad says, his voice full of emotion. "I'm so, so, proud."

"Thanks, Dad," I say, wiping the snot and tears from my face.

I really needed to hear it from him. He always tells me he's proud of me but until now I don't think I believed in myself enough to believe him.

I stop to give my sister and mam kisses before climbing back on stage to stand with my cast in my spot between Katie and

Zach, both of whom take my hands for one last tearful bow.

When we exit the stage, most of the crew are waiting for us, every single person backstage has tears streaming down their face, most of them had no idea my dad was so poorly, it's not like I go around advertising the fact.

After a lot of hugs are exchanged, most people clear out to get changed and all I want is to see Liam. When I spot him, he opens his arms and beckons me to him. I don't hesitate to snuggle into his warm body, wrapping my arms around his waist and holding onto him tightly. I don't care that Diane is only a few metres away watching us, I don't even glance her way to acknowledge it and neither does Liam, she's not ruining this for us.

CHAPTER TWENTY
Liam

With Harriet's family safely escorted to the dress circle bar, I make my way backstage again to help reset for tomorrow's performance. Everyone I encounter on my way is ecstatic with how the show went, laughter and joy fill the corridors as we celebrate a job well done.

This adrenaline rush is why I love working in theatre. Everyone came together tonight to work incredibly hard, and it all paid off because the show was a success.

"That was a really nice thing you did for Harriet's family, kid," Di says, sidling up next to me where I'm sorting props, making sure they're all where they're supposed to be.

"They deserve it, life's been pretty shitty for them lately."

"Yeah, I get that. After what happened to your mam, I'm sure it's hard for you to see someone else go through the same thing."

"Yeah," I agree but don't expand, not trusting where this is going. I know she saw us at the end, and I know she'll have an opinion.

"You know we're keeping you and Harriet apart for your

own good, right?" she says, echoing the statement she made when I first met Harriet.

"I don't see how my boss dictating something in my personal life is for my own good, do you?"

"He's your dad, Liam, he wants what's best for you. I want what's best for you." Her voice is calm and soothing, but something in it doesn't sit right.

"He might be my father but… do you know, I can't actually remember the last conversation we had. Anything he needs to tell me he sends you, so I highly doubt this is about what's best for me, more like controlling me."

Diane doesn't react. "Does she know who your dad is? Have you told her?" she asks carefully.

"No, I've not told her."

"What do you think she'd do if she knew? What do you think her reaction will be when she finds out your name is carved into stone at the theatre entrance? That your dad signs her payslip each month. We're protecting you from being used because we know that will happen. That's why we kept you out of the limelight growing up, it's why we kept you a secret. We were protecting you then and we're protecting you now. Have I ever done anything that has given you cause to doubt me?" she insists.

And there it is, my worst fear laid out bare in front of me.

Would Harriet use me to try and get ahead, not knowing that I can't grant her anything? Hell, I can't even see or speak to my own dad so it's not like I can get anyone else access to him. But that's what happens when people find out I'm the son of a Whitton.

They'll think I'm a stepping stone to him so they can get ahead in this world.

As soon as the thought enters my mind, I scold myself because Harriet isn't like that, and I don't believe for a second she would do such a thing.

"Just keep that in mind and remember that out of everyone here, I'm the only person you can trust." With that, she leaves. I'm alone, sorting props and trying not to let the doubts and fear crush me, because although I know it's nonsense, being suspicious has been ingrained in me since I was a kid.

CHAPTER TWENTY-ONE
Harriet

Last night, I had my last performance in the lead role before Rachael returns and to celebrate a whole month since opening night, the company put on a boozy afternoon tea with finger sandwiches, delicate cakes and champagne in the dress circle bar.

Everyone is looking forward to some much-needed rest as the show closes for a week before we embark on another four-week run. After that, we'll have another week off, then the final four weeks. It's not standard practice but as the show is new and this run is like a pilot, the production decided to try something different before our Sunderland residency ends and we embark on a national tour.

When Liam returns from the bar, he takes Jayne's seat next to me and rests his sculpted arms along the back of the booth behind me. When his rough calloused fingertips graze my shoulder, a shiver of desire ripples from the top of my head to the tip of my toes.

"I want to show you something." he says, leaning in so close that goosebumps prickle down my neck at the feel of his breath on my sensitive skin. We've been on our best behaviour lately and have let our friendship develop below the radar for the most part.

"What is it?"

"It's easier if I show you. Meet me down by the stage in five minutes." With no further indication what this is all about, he stands casually and leaves the room.

I let a few minutes pass, then stand and exit the bar through a different door, without saying a word to anyone. But by the look on our friends faces, they clearly know something is going on. As I walk through the maze of corridors, I keep my wits about me, going up a floor on one staircase, along a corridor and then down two floors so I know I'm not being followed.

Okay, yeah, I know I'm being a bit OTT, but we still have to be careful.

It's dark when I reach backstage, only the ghost light illuminating a small area of the stage, so I can't see anything. Some of the scenery has been removed from the area for repairs/touch-ups so the stage is a black cavern again.

"Liam?" I whisper as I creep around in the darkness.

"I'm right here." I squeal at the fright. "Sorry," he adds, making noise so I know he's coming up behind me. His strong hands caress my hips, and he pulls me into him, so my back is flush with his front.

I relax into him on instinct even though it's been weeks since he last held me on opening night.

"You scared the living daylights out of me."

Turning in his arms to face him, I swat his chest jovially

and he laughs through an apology. I can just make out his face in the shadows, but every passing second, he becomes clearer as my eyes adjust.

His laughter trails off as we stand together in the darkness, his arms locked securely around my body. We hold each other in a short period of loaded silence, too afraid to let each other go because if we do, we'll have to go back to pretending our feelings aren't real.

"Is this what you wanted to show me?" I ask, sliding my hands up his chest until I can wrap them around his broad shoulders, letting my fingertips caress the nape of his neck.

"No, come with me," he says, taking my hand and leading me out onto the empty stage.

Liam

Although the stage is only lit by the ghost light, the auditorium still has the safety lights on. The deep red and gold tones set the ambience and when I turn to face Harriet, she looks out in amazement, as if she's seeing the theatre for the first time.

"No matter how many times I step out onto this stage, it always feels like the first time. I'll never take this view for granted," she says, grinning at me as I watch her.

"Me neither," I say, because seeing Harriet so completely happy in her element is a memory I'll treasure forever. "I wanted to show you my favourite part of the theatre."

"The stage is your favourite part?" she asks,

understandably confused. "You hate attention."

"Right here, this is my favourite." I lead her to the exact centre of the stage, telling her to lie down.

"Lie down?" she asks confused.

"Trust me." I'm well aware I have no right to ask that of her when I still haven't been a hundred per cent honest with her in the time we've known each other. There have been plenty of opportunities to tell her all about my dad, to confess everything, but the longer this goes on, the more scared I become that by telling her, I'll lose her.

I let go of her hand and lie on the floor on my back. She smiles and does the same as if it's not weird that I've brought her to an empty stage and asked her to lie on a dusty floor since the stage hasn't had a deep clean since the Get In.

"That," I say, pointing to the fly system above us, "that's my favourite part."

From the auditorium the stage looks small and compact, but the reality is quite different. The stage extends upwards where an intricate design of illuminated wires and beams form the fly system.

"It's pretty amazing," she agrees. I can feel her eyes on me again. "I don't think I've ever really took the time to look up."

"It always amazes me how large the stage is when nothing is on the ground. The space is so vast, but we only ever allow the audience to see a tiny snippet, kind of like our true selves. We show enough of ourselves to tell the story we want to, keeping other things hidden in the fly tower until we're ready to show them," I say, using it as a metaphor for the secrets I'm keeping.

133

"That's beautiful…" she pauses. "You know, you can tell me anything, right. Whatever is going on with you and Diane, you can tell me."

Of course, Harriet has noticed the increasing tension between Diane and me. As the weeks go on, the control I'm under has started to dissolve the more I'm aware of it. Diane has noticed too; it's only a matter of time before things really come to a head.

I tuck my arm furthest from her behind my neck to form a cushion between me and the floor. With her back still flat on the ground, she turns her head to the side to look at me, reaching over to squeeze my hand in a gesture so warm and comforting I never want her to let me go. I turn my head, mirroring her, and the words spill out.

"Diane is my dad's best friend," I say.

"Oh," she says, understanding. It's not the first time I've mentioned I have issues with him.

"I told you I didn't meet him until I was seven, but even then, he wasn't around much, he was always away for business. He paid the bare minimum amount for child support and told me I'd have to work and earn my own money to pay for my education. He got me a job here selling popcorn and refreshments from a cart in the entrance and always uses that as leverage. I can't be disappointed that he's not around because he got me my first job, and my second, third, fourth etc. He got me this job too."

"Do you see him now?"

"I haven't seen him for years. There's more to it, but… that's the part I'm struggling with, Harriet. I wish more than anything I had the words to tell you everything, but I don't right now."

"That's okay, you don't need to tell me," she says, comfortingly.

"I will one day, I promise."

"Thank you for talking to me and for showing me your favourite place." Her voice is soft and sweet and for the first time in three weeks, I do something risky and guide her to me so her head is resting on my chest like I'm a pillow. I let myself hold her and pretend everything is fine as my hand traces patterns down the exposed skin of her waist below her cropped t-shirt. She lets out a content sigh as she rests her petite hand on my pec, and I smile.

The only sounds to be heard are the sounds of our breathing. It's a welcome reprieve from everything else going on in our world.

CHAPTER TWENTY-TWO
Liam

Harriet is usually very vocal – she communicates everything to me and it's something I love most about her – so, now that she's silent, I'm desperate to know what's running through her mind. Since we've opened the floodgates and are allowing this physical closeness, is she imagining a world where this is normal for us like I am? Is the blood rushing around her veins a million miles an hour like mine is or is she calm and collected inside?

In the show there's a love song, an internal monologue where the heroine wants to tell the hero she loves him but can't because they don't live in a world where they can be together. It's fitting to our situation, so I whistle the tune aloud to her now.

Harriet gasps and I laugh because it's not the song choice that has her shocked.

"You aren't allowed to whistle in a theatre, especially not on stage."

I chuckle because she's deadly serious and it's adorable. "Theatre folk are so superstitious."

"You aren't superstitious?" She props herself up onto her elbow so she's looking down at me and it takes everything, absolutely everything, inside me not to pull her down on top of me and bring her lips to mine.

If she makes a move tonight, I'm all hers, no doubt about it.

"I don't go walking under ladders or anything. But that's more about safety than anything else, just like you shouldn't whistle in a theatre is for safety. I do humour some of the superstitions. I once said the name of 'That Scottish Play' and the director at the time made me go outside, spin around three times and spit before I could come back in. It was a little embarrassing; the crew recorded it and put it on YouTube. Besides, when you mess with superstitions, it puts the actors in a terrible mood."

"You know, in *Hamilton*, Alexander Hamilton actually mentions the play by name, or rather he references the title character."

"*Hamilton* is one of the biggest productions in the world right now and nothing bad has happened. Doesn't that prove we aren't all going to be cursed by uttering a single word?"

"Possibly, but, in the show, after Alexander Hamilton mentions it in the letter to Angelica, that's when it all goes downhill for him."

"Coincidence?" I laugh.

"I don't think anything Lin Manuel Miranda does is a coincidence." I'm well aware of the love she has for him. "The man is a genius. They also wear a lot of blue in *Hamilton*. Which is another superstition, although less common these days, but it really feels like Lin is testing the boundaries of superstition."

"Want to know my favourite superstition?" I ask.

"Of course."

"The ghost light," I answer, looking at the standing floor light in the middle of the stage. "I like the idea that the ghosts come out to perform at night."

She smiles. "What do you say, Nancy? You want to come dance with us?"

When she's met with nothing but silence, I shrug.

"Maybe she has stage fright. After all, she died on stage," she reasons.

"You'd pass out if she appeared, wouldn't you?" I laugh.

"Oh, absolutely. No doubt about that."

We fall into a contemplative silence when she lies back down, snuggling into me as I continue to brush my fingers across her skin, absorbing the buzzing atmosphere of the empty auditorium.

"What was Harriet Adams like in drama school?" I ask.

"I loved everything about it. I was always reading and researching and learning about all thing's theatre, when some kids just wanted to be a star. I read every textbook we were given, and I became weirdly obsessed with theatre facts. As you're aware, I still love a good fact."

"Your random theatre facts are still the highlight of my day. They're the things I look forward to most." A faint blush paints her cheeks. "What's your favourite thing about performing?"

"At the moment, performing is a distraction. When I stand in the wings and get into character, everything that's going on in my life disappears and I'm someone else. Yes, this character has her issues, but at the end of the night she gets her happily ever after and when I'm in the moment, it feels like I'll get my happily ever after too. Throughout the show, I don't get a chance to think about life or what's happening outside of that moment. I'm always thinking about the very next step, the next dance move or the next line. I guess it's why I like being a swing, I have to concentrate on whichever track I'm covering, so there's no room for anything else, no room for any difficult thoughts."

I lift my hand up to stroke her hair, leaning down and pressing a kiss to the top of her head.

"Do you enjoy your job?" She props herself up once more to look down at me, her rich chocolate hair tumbling in waves to the side where she's released it from her bobble.

"I wish I could say I do, but right now I feel stuck in a rut. I've been up for promotion for years now and keep getting passed over. I don't know, I've never said this aloud before, but what if it's because I'm not as good as I think I am? What if that's the reason I don't get promoted."

"Without you this production would fall apart. You're so hard on yourself. Believe me when I say you're amazing at what you do. Don't let anyone tell you otherwise. I see the difference you make, everyone in the cast and crew does too. Diane may be the stage manager, but you are the one propping everyone up night after night without complaint. I truly mean it when I say I don't think I would enjoy this experience as much if you weren't here supporting me every second of the day."

"I could say the same about you. It's like you were meant to be here." I look deep into her eyes, cupping her face with my hand, allowing myself to savour this moment.

CHAPTER TWENTY-THREE
Liam

Harriet looks at her watch and groans.

"We should get back to the party before someone notices we're not there."

She's right, we've been gone a while now and I know Di will have noticed, but I don't want to leave. She stands and I mirror her, but she doesn't look like she's fully convinced herself to leave just yet.

Sensing her reluctance, I decide to play devil's advocate. "What if we stayed?"

"I'm worried that if I stay, I'll do something I shouldn't." Her eyes drop to my mouth.

"What if I want you to?" I step closer to her, my voice low and husky. Christ, I want her, and I'm done trying to fight this. "I don't think being friends is enough for me anymore, Harriet."

"Liam…" My name spills from her lips on a sigh. I can't quite tell if she's warning me off or pleading with me to make the first move, so I stand there silent, not knowing what to do. "We really shouldn't." She answers my unspoken question although she looks torn.

"Shit… No, you're right. I'm sorry." I take two steps back and so does she, crossing her arms and then uncrossing them when she realises all that motion does is push up her boobs, making her look even more tempting.

"Although…" she says slowly. Harriet showing that tiny second of doubt is enough to have my spirits soaring.

"How about a pros and cons list?"

She nods enthusiastically. "Great idea! Start with the cons?" This time I'm the one nodding like the Churchill dog. "Firstly, our careers. That's a big risk for us to take, we could lose our jobs."

"That's a pretty good reason not to act on this. Any more cons to us getting together?"

"There's also the fact…" She thinks for a moment for another con but comes up short. "Or, you know…"

"What about…" I try and nothing comes to mind for me either. "I've got nothing."

"I think about you all the time." She looks at her feet. Glancing up at me from below her thick lashes, she adds, "I think about you when I go to sleep, about all the ways you're good for me. I've been hurt before by someone I trusted, but I know you wouldn't hurt me." She takes a tentative half step closer to me, and I mirror her, reducing the distance between us ever so slightly. My heart speeds up with excitement, with need.

"We have the same interests, the same likes and dislikes," I continue our pros list, both of us taking another small step closer to one another.

"We make each other laugh, all the time," she adds, initiating another step forward.

"I hate the gherkins on a McDonald's double cheeseburger, and you love them. If that doesn't scream perfect for each other, I don't know what does." That one earns me a sweet laugh from her. "You build me up. I don't even think you know you're doing it, but you make me feel like I'm ten feet tall just by looking at me." The tension is hanging thick between us, the physical distance between us is barely inches now.

"Being your friend, it's not enough for me anymore either," she says echoing my earlier sentiment and my resolve breaks.

"I'm done fighting this, Harriet. I'm ready to give in. Are you?"

Our breathing is heavy in anticipation, as if we're being pulled together with every breath.

"Not giving in might kill me." Her soft pink lips are plump and parted, begging to be kissed. I can't keep my eyes off them. When she chews nervously on her bottom lip, it almost sends me over the edge. My heart is beating rapidly in my chest, matching the rise and fall of hers. I'm so far gone for this girl I can barely think straight at the prospect of kissing her.

I tangle my fingers through her hair to her nape. Placing my other palm against the side of her neck, my thumb traces a line up her slender throat to her jaw, tilting her face upwards. I need the green light from her.

"We could keep it a secret. They can't sack us if they don't know about it," she says, and I nod, my nose brushing against hers, nudging her affectionately.

"I want this, Harriet, I want us," I say, my voice a hoarse whisper. "I want you so bad it hurts. My teeth hurt."

She laughs as I use her vivid description from all those weeks ago.

Using the hand that's pressed against her neck, I position her so I can brush my lips against the smooth warm skin of her jaw and down her neck. She lets out a sigh of desire when I bring my other hand to the base of her spine and pull her closer. There's no distance left between us. My heart is pounding when she slides her palms up my chest and around my neck.

"I know deep inside this is a bad idea," I say as she relaxes into my kiss, gasping as my beard scratches at her neck. "Do you want me to stop?"

"Do not fucking stop!" Her fingers dig into my shoulders. I smile and return my lips to her neck, my thumb traces down her throat and she moans. She fucking moans and I almost die on the spot.

"This might be a bad idea, but it's a really good, bad idea," she says as I kiss to the left of her mouth. She whimpers in frustration, and I groan like some wild tortured animal. I wanted to drag this out, to savour it, but I'm getting desperate now so when she pleads with me to kiss her, I grin and lower my mouth to hers.

Our lips meet in a passionate embrace as we attempt to release a month's worth of pent-up sexual tension in one second, but just as I pull her impossibly closer, intending to deepen our kiss, we're interrupted by the loud opening and closing of a door.

We scramble away from each other, contemplating if there's enough time to hide, although we both know there isn't.

As Harriet presses her swollen lips, her eyes wide in panic, Di appears with a stern frown as she glares between us, clearly putting the pieces together. Our secret lasted all of five seconds.

"What are you two doing in here?"

"Harriet forgot her jacket and was too afraid of the ghosts, so I escorted her so she wouldn't be frightened," I come up with.

Harriet nods in agreement as she holds up my hoody in her hand, but even I can see the guilty look on her face. Her lips are plump and her cheeks are flushed. There's a carnal look in her eyes, one I'm sure is in mine too, a tell-tale sign that we were just up to no good.

"Liam. Can you help me look for my phone charger? I'll check here, can you check the fly bridge?" Di asks, although it's more of an order than a question.

"Why on earth would your phone charger be up—"

"You can do that alone, right? I know you aren't afraid of the ghosts."

I feel a surge of anger towards her. It takes everything I have not to turn into a petulant child and stomp my feet.

"Of course," I say, clenching my jaw.

"Harriet, why don't go back to the party? A lot of people are specifically here to see you this afternoon." Diane looks pointedly at Harriet.

"Sorry, Diane. I'll see you both out there," she says, giving me a tight-lipped smile. "Thank you for coming with me." She

145

glances between me and Di, and I can see in her expression she doesn't want to leave us, but I give her an encouraging nod before she exits the stage.

"There is no phone charger, is there?" I ask when the door closes behind Harriet.

"A bit of space will do you good over the next week. I've warned you, if this continues, I'll have to involve your dad and none of us want that."

"God forbid, my dad gets involved. You know what, you should call him. Maybe I'll see him this decade if that's the case!" I yell, but before she can respond, I storm off the stage in the same direction Harriet went a few seconds earlier. Instead of going back to the party, I turn the opposite way towards the stage door, needing some fresh air.

Two more months, that's all I have left here, and then I'll finally be free.

CHAPTER TWENTY-FOUR

Harriet

My eyes flit between the door and the grandfather clock beside it for half an hour before I decide it's time to leave. He obviously isn't coming back.

I check my phone and there's nothing from him. Did he have second thoughts and leave?

"I'm going to go home, I'm not feeling great," I say to Jayne, feeling deflated more than anything. "You stay though, I'll get the bus home," I add when I notice her sorry glance at Katie.

All those people that came specifically to see me soon cleared out once the cakes were cleared away so there really is no need for me to hang around moping any longer than I have been.

"Are you sure? I'll come with you. I don't have to stay."

"No, don't be daft. Stay and have fun." I pat her arm, trying my best to disguise my low mood. Someone deserves to be happy tonight. Katie gives me an appreciative smile. I'm not sure if anything has happened between them yet, but they definitely look closer today.

I say goodbye to my friends and tell them I'll see them when we return in a week. Since a lot of the cast and crew have come from other areas of the country, they're looking forward to seeing their families and friends again after being away for so long.

I take my time walking through the hallways just like I have done a hundred times the past month. When I push through the door to the green room, I find Liam lying on his back across one of the well-worn, brown leather sofas with his air pods in. He doesn't notice me until I'm leaning over his head that's resting on the arm of the sofa.

He jumps up quickly when he notices me, pulling his headphones out and putting them in his pocket.

"I thought you had left." My heart swells, he waited for me.

"Without you? No way. I couldn't face going back there so thought I'd wait for you here. I didn't want you to feel pressure to leave before you were ready, so I waited… It sounds creepy when I say it aloud. Are you leaving?"

"Yeah, Jayne is staying with Katie, so I was going to get the bus home." I hitch my bag further up my shoulder as it slips down my arm.

"I'll drive you," he says eagerly, getting to his feet. He takes my heavy bag from me and carries it with ease.

It's mid-afternoon when we exit stage door. The sun is still high and bright, which always catches me by surprise when I emerge from the enclosed hallways of backstage. The heatwave passed a couple of weeks ago, but it's still been nice and warm during the day.

Together we walk in a companionable silence and when we're a safe enough distance from the theatre, he slips his hand into mine and we grin happily at each other like lovesick teenagers.

When we reach Liam's car, he opens the door, leans down and presses a soft kiss to my lips. When he pulls back, he glances at his watch. "It's only four o'clock, do you want to hang out a little more?"

I'm back to grinning like an idiot. "I'd love to." I pull him in closer to deepen our kiss nowhere near ready for this to end. "Why don't we go back to your place?"

CHAPTER TWENTY-FIVE
Liam

"It's not much," I tell her as I open the door and lead Harriet through the small hallway of my cottage.

"Do I get the tour?" she asks, looking around the small entrance hall as we take off our shoes and set them side by side.

"Follow me."

As I give her a tour around the kitchen and living room, I tell her all about my plans to renovate one day soon and she listens with rapt attention.

"Where do you sleep?"

"I'll show you." I take her hand and lead her upstairs to the loft conversion. "This is my room."

She walks in and looks around as I stand in the doorframe, trying to see it through her eyes. My white bedding is freshly washed, and the bed is made for a change, thank god. I wasn't expecting to bring her back here. Hoping? Always. Expecting? No.

She wanders around the room, looking at the books and DVDs lining the shelves. She stops when she comes to the framed photos on top of my chest of drawers, so I join her, standing closely behind her.

"That's me and Katie when we were little. And that's me and my mam."

"She was beautiful."

I nod, unable to articulate the thoughts running through my mind.

I take the photo from her and place it back where it belongs. Knowing it's exactly what I need, she wraps her arms around my neck and looks deep into my eyes. Rubbing her palms against my nape, she comforts me.

I've never felt this way about a woman, sure, there have been others in the past, but any feelings I had for them don't come close to what I feel for Harriet.

Before Harriet, I'd never met anyone that made me think to myself *I wish I could tell my mam about her.*

There was an episode of *Sabrina the Teenage Witch* that I remember so vividly from my childhood where Sabrina had a chance to meet with someone she loved who had passed on. Katie used to watch it when we were younger. I'd never really pay attention, I'd be too busy trying to 'catch 'em all' on my Gameboy, but this one day, I sat with her and watched it.

After Mam died, I used to think that if I had ten minutes to speak to her again, I'd ask for her advice on how to get out of this torturous cycle I'm in with my dad, because she would know exactly what to do. Now, I know I'd tell her about Harriet. I'd tell her that I've met a woman so incredibly beautiful, kind and loving. A woman who makes me the happiest I've been in a long time. A woman I'm pretty sure I want to spend my life with; who I want to build a family with.

I'd tell her that, above all odds, this woman is choosing me too and that it kills me to know they'll never get to meet.

I've never met a woman I would give absolutely everything up for, but I know if being with Harriet means I need to leave and find a new job, I'd do it in a heartbeat. Hell, I'd walk in there on Monday morning and quit on the spot if she asked me to. I'd do it even if she didn't ask me to; the only thing stopping me is that I know she wouldn't want that.

"My mam would love you so much," I say, finally breaking the silence between us. "It kills me that she'll never get to meet you."

"Oh, Liam." She wraps her arms around me tighter. I grip onto her too, around her waist, and bury my face in her neck, seeking comfort in the fruity scent of her shampoo.

She holds me until I can pull myself together.

"I'm falling in love with you, Harriet," I say honestly. I know it's too early to be declaring my love for her, but that's exactly what this is.

"I'm falling in love with you too."

I let out a relieved laugh because I can't believe how lucky I am to have her say that to me and know she means it.

This time when we kiss, it's slow and tentative. We take our time because we know there's no way we're going to be caught. There's no reason to rush this or stumble around.

We slowly make our way to my bed, and she pulls me down on top of her as we kiss.

She opens up to me, brushing her tongue against mine as we explore and caress each other, as much as we can with our clothes on, until we're both breathing hard, the anticipation almost too much.

"Liam," she pleads with me as I press into her, my body aching for friction. She gasps and grinds against me, finding my erection through my jeans. I push my hand up her thigh, taking her light summer dress with it and pressing into her harder.

"Is this okay?"

She nods. "I've never been so sure about anything in my life. I need more."

I stand and hold out my hand to help her up so I can pull her dress over her head tossing it on the floor closely followed by my t-shirt. Reaching for my belt she undoes the buckle and opens the fly of my jeans, her fingertips leaving a trail of heat where she brushes them over the skin of my stomach. We continue undressing each other slowly between passionate kisses, savouring the moment until there's nothing left between us.

"You're so beautiful," I whisper in her ear before my mouth brushes soft kisses along her jaw and down her neck. A shiver runs down her spine as her nipples pucker and she lets out a pleasurable sigh. I'm desperate to pull one into my mouth and see what reaction I'm rewarded with, but as torturous as it is for me, I hold back.

I brush the length of her spine with my hand until I get to the dip at the base and place my palm against it, pulling her closer to me.

Picking her up with my hands under her bum, I kiss her

again as I carry her back to bed, placing her head gently on my pillow.

"Your bed smells like you," she says, as I lie between her legs, the tip of my excruciatingly hard dick brushing her entrance. I can feel how wet she is against the head and it's a tough battle to keep control and not blow it before we've even begun.

"Is that a good thing?"

"I wish I could bottle it and take it home with me."

I laugh softly. "You could always stay."

"That's why you're the brains." She gasps on the last word as I stroke down her stomach and over her pubic bone. I move back slightly so I can sweep my fingers over the sensitive flesh between her legs, groaning in pleasure at exactly how ready she is for me.

She reaches between us too as I continue my slow pace of stroking her. She wraps her delicate hand around my aching length, gripping it as she glides her fist back and forth and back and forth as pleasure rips through me. I pull my own hand back to still hers knowing that if she continues, this is going to be over before we know it.

"Can I go down on you?" I want to know I'm not pushing any boundaries.

"I'd love it, but I know some men don't like it, so you don't have to if you don't want to." She sounds self-conscious.

"Babe, I want to."

I don't just want to, I'm desperate to.

"You're not just saying that? If you want to stop—"

"Harriet, I don't want to stop until I hear you screaming my name and feel you come on my tongue. Believe me when I say I'll get as much enjoyment out of doing this as you will, you'll see."

"Oh fuck," she whispers against my mouth as I tease her clit again with my fingers, a dark desire settling in her eyes.

Working my way down her body, I kiss and lick her sensitive skin, making a mental note of what makes her gasp and moan. When I finally draw a perfect, pink nipple into my mouth, her back arches off the bed and when I take the other between my forefinger and thumb, her hands fist the sheets by her side.

"Liam," she gasps.

"That's it, Harriet."

I think back to all those weeks ago when I watched her act this out on stage – she didn't look like this. This is way more expressive and intimate. This is for me only, not a theatrical performance and, fuck, it makes me ecstatic.

I swap to her other nipple, pulling it into my mouth, sucking on the hard nub before circling it with my tongue. I groan happily when her fingers tangle in my hair and she tugs gently on the strands.

When I look up at her, she's watching me, her eyes clouded with desire. I lap my tongue against her nipple one last time before continuing my descent, drawing out her pleasure as much as I can.

I slide further down the bed, getting comfortable as I reach the apex of her thighs. I widen her legs further, hooking one over my shoulder and using my fingers to open her up to me for the first time.

Fuck, she's perfect.

My dick throbs at the sight of her, desperate to claim her.

I can't take my eyes off her as I use my fingers to brush through her folds and push against her glistening opening. She leans up on her elbows to watch me enter her. I watch her face as I push my finger deep inside of her for the first time, she hangs her head back and moans.

"Do you like that, Harriet?" I ask, my voice hoarse with restraint.

"Oh fuck! Yes," she cries out.

I could get addicted to watching her like this.

I slowly pump a finger into her until she's ready for a second, and then I bring my mouth down to her with a long brush of my tongue.

"Oh, shit. You taste amazing," I say on a moan as I do my best to slow down. All I want to do is devour her, to lap up every last drop of her as soon as possible, but judging by her earlier statement, she's never experienced a man get so much pleasure from doing this to her. So that's what I want to show her, that I'm loving this as much as she is.

I listen to every sound she makes, pay attention to every swirl of her hips and every tug of my hair, learning what she likes. I moan against her as I stroke her from the inside, revelling in the moment. The little moans and gasps she made when I kissed her for the first time are amplified and I love how vocal she is, letting me know how much she enjoys this. It's a turn on and an ego boost in one.

"Oh my god!" She cries out as I increase the pressure and

speed of my tongue. "Liam! Yes! Right there."

Unable to hold back, I grip my dick in my hand and stroke, doing this to her is enough to make me come too.

With the hand that's not buried in my hair, she pinches her nipples, gasping from the sensation.

"I'm so close," she cries.

"Come for me, Harriet. Don't hold back."

As I coax the orgasm from her with my tongue and pound into her with my fingers, I can feel her walls tighten around them, a tell-tale sign that she's close. I swirl my tongue around her clit and suck it into my mouth, rolling it between my lips and letting go again, continuing the cycle as we both moan in pleasure.

Fuck, I'm so close to coming myself, I won't be able to hold off much longer.

"Liam! Oh, fuck! Liam! Yes!" she cries out and with one hand still tangled in my hair, her back arches from the bed again, gathering the quilt in her other white knuckled fist. The second I feel her climax clamping down on my fingers, my balls tighten and I come in my hand with a carnal roar, white hot pleasure blinding me.

Slowly withdrawing my fingers, I synchronise my languid licks against her clenching flesh to my own strokes as we ride out the final moments of our orgasms together. Once our bodies recover enough to move, I jump up and grab a towel to clean up.

"Did you...?" she asks, propping herself up on her elbows, watching me throw the towel in the washing basket.

I nod. "I told you I'd get as much out of that as you did." I grin as I pull the blanket over us, bringing her in closer to me and kissing her lazily.

We lie like this for a while, all tangled up and holding each other. We caress each other and whisper sweet nothings until her breathing eventually evens out and a tiny, satisfied sigh slips through her lips. When I know she's asleep, I kiss the tip of her nose and close my eyes, letting myself drift off with her.

CHAPTER TWENTY-SIX
Harriet

The smell of pizza wafts through the air as I slowly return to the land of the living. I reach out for Liam and find his side of the bed warm but empty, meaning he can't have been up long.

I have no idea where my phone is to check the time and, like most people our age, Liam doesn't have an actual clock in his room. Deciding I should probably get up, I look around until my eyes land on his t-shirt and I pull it on. I can't see my underwear anywhere but fuck it, I don't need it anyway.

I follow the smell of food into his kitchen and find him shirtless, wearing a pair of shorts as he leans down to check the oven.

Leaning on the doorframe and crossing my arms over my chest, I watch his tight back muscles tense and release with his movements. I can't help it. The man gave me the most intense orgasm of my life and enjoyed it himself. If I weren't already head over heels in love with him, that would have clinched it.

"Are you enjoying the show?" he asks without turning to look at me.

"You have no idea." I stand behind him and wind my arms

around his torso, kissing between his shoulder blades and resting my head against his warm back. I plant my palms on his pecs, getting a good grope. He lets out a low chuckle and turns in my arms so he can bend his neck to kiss me.

"Good nap?"

"The best, I needed it that's for sure."

He kisses me again before returning to the pizza. "I thought you might be hungry, so I threw this in the oven."

"I'm famished. I feel like I've had a good workout and I didn't do anything!"

"Oh, believe me, you did a lot," he says with a naughty tone. "Help yourself to a drink out of the fridge. I'll serve this up before it goes cold."

I go to the fridge, pull out a bottle of Diet Coke and pour us both a glass, setting them on his round wooden kitchen table. He brings the pizza over and places it in the middle.

"What time is it?" I ask when he sits across from me, placing two plates in front of us.

"Just after seven."

"Wow, I thought we'd been asleep for hours."

"Only about an hour, and then your grumbling tummy woke me up."

"Ah, so you're well trained when it comes to hungry females then?"

"I grew up with Katie, it was either learn quickly or face her wrath."

I can't help but laugh and so does he. "You guys have the

cutest relationship." He always talks about Katie fondly, even when he is taking the piss out of her.

"We've always been close, more like siblings. Don't get me wrong, I love her deeply, but we spent a lot of our childhood fighting. She's younger than me, so when I was going through my awkward teen years, I didn't really want her hanging around and that's all she seemed to want to do. We became friends in adulthood though and honestly, I don't think I could live without her." After losing his mam and his dad being a prick, I'm glad he has Katie.

"I guess that's the good thing about me and Jayne being so close in age, we've always been friends, and we've always understood one another. As you've witnessed, she can be a huge annoying pain in my arse, but I suppose that's her job as the little sister."

"Maybe that's what makes them so good for each other."

I nod my agreement.

I take a bite of pizza and my eyes roll back in my head at how good it tastes. I mean, it's a basic oven pizza, but right now it's the single greatest thing I've ever tasted.

"Annnnnd, I'm hard again," Liam says, adjusting his shorts.

I laugh. "Down boy, I need to get my energy back up again if we're going to fit another round in before I have to go."

He smiles. It's funny how comfortable we are talking about this; my previous boyfriends haven't wanted to talk openly about pleasure and sex. Before today, I don't even think I've had sex in the daylight, never mind had such an open conversation about it.

My most recent ex hated anything other than bog-standard penetration, and god forbid I ask him to go down on me. I know it's all about what we're comfortable with, and the sex could be good at times, and obviously, he's well within his rights to say no, but it was just another glaring factor telling me that we weren't at all compatible that I ignored until it was much too late.

After we finish the pizza, I stand at the sink and attempt to wash up as he stands behind me roaming his hands over my body, kissing my neck and tweaking my nipples through the thin fabric of his t-shirt.

"This morning, when you woke up, would you have guessed we'd be here now?" he asks, his mouth close to my ear.

"Never in a million years, but I'm so happy we are." I gasp as he presses his erection into the small of my back. I want him. It's barely been two hours since he gave me a mind-melting orgasm and I'm desperate for a second.

"You look incredible wearing my t-shirt," he says, this time nipping my earlobe with his teeth, causing a thrill to ripple down my spine and settle between my legs.

"I'm not wearing any underwear." I breathe out, gripping the edge of the sink as he continues to play with my nipples, the washing up long forgotten.

He redirects his attention from one of my breasts and runs his fingers up the back of my thighs, nudging my feet apart with his foot, so there's room for him to slide his fingers over me from behind.

"Oh shit." My head lolls forward. The hand he's using to

toy with my nipples travels up to my throat, bringing my head back to rest on his collarbone so he can kiss the sensitive skin on my neck.

"I imagined myself doing this to you that first microphone fitting," he says, his voice low and seductive. "I came home that night and replayed that fantasy repeatedly. It's something I think about often."

I whimper when he rolls my clit through his fingers. I open my legs wider for him, but he doesn't enter me, instead he spreads my moisture over me as my hips move of their own accord.

"I want you, Liam. I want you inside of me right here."

I reach around and grab him in my fist. He's rock solid and ready to go. He moans as I grip him. Letting go and using both of my hands, I push his shorts to the floor. He isn't wearing any underwear either.

"I didn't bring any protection downstairs with me, can you wait here?"

"I'm on the pill and I'm clean... I got tested recently."

"Are you sure? I'm clean too, but I don't mind wearing a condom if you'd feel safer."

"I trust you." I mean it. He's the only man I've ever considered doing this with.

He turns me around to face him and kisses me hard, then picks me up effortlessly to stride across the kitchen to his chair, sitting down with me on his lap. He lifts the hem of his shirt and peels it off me, tossing it aside so I'm naked on top of him.

I can feel his tip pressing against me and I just need to

adjust my hips ever so slightly until he's lined up perfectly. I take his face in my hands and kiss him as I slowly sink down onto his hard length for the first time. Our moans fill the air as my body stretches around him. I feel so full as I lift myself up and slide down him again and again, taking him deeper each time until our bases meet.

"You feel so good, Harriet." He moans as his teeth graze my neck, his trimmed beard grazing my skin in the most wonderful way as he kisses down me my chest. "It's like you're made for me.

He pulls a nipple into his mouth and tweaks the other, adding yet more wonderful sensations to the mix. When I start to move my hips, rocking against him, my clit rubs against his pubic bone and, holy fuck, if this isn't the best feeling in the world.

The sounds of our pleasure fill the air as Liam takes control. His fingers bite into me as he helps me move my hips while thrusting up into me.

"I need it harder," I beg.

"Whatever you need, babe. I'll give it to you."

Without pulling out, Liam stands, planting me on the edge of the table so I'm sitting in a reclined position, bracing myself with a palm on the oak beneath me and the other at the back of his neck. I didn't think he could get any deeper, but this new angle opens me up further for him as he drives into me harder.

"How's that?" he asks, and I love that even in the throes of passion he's thinking about me and my pleasure.

"Just like that," I cry out as he pounds into me harder and harder, exactly the way I need it. The table creaks and groans under the impact of our bodies slamming together, but I'm not worried because before long my orgasm is building and all I care about is this man right here. Nothing else exists in this moment other than the two of us in a vacuum somewhere in the universe.

"Fuck, Harriet. I love the way you take me," he growls, a moan forming from deep within him.

As I hurtle towards the finish line, I can tell Liam is holding back on his own pleasure, he's waiting for me to come first. His entire body is tense, his muscles straining. He doesn't need to hold on for long because I'm right there, seconds from combustion.

He pulls his thumb into his mouth before reaching between us to brush against my clit.

"I'm coming! Fuck, Liam, I'm coming!" I know he likes it when I scream his name, so I do it again for good measure as he grunts out more deliciously filthy encouragement as my body clamps down around him. My vision blurs, my orgasm hitting harder than it ever has before.

After a few more hard thrusts, he stills inside me with a loud "fuck," as he reaches his own crescendo. I can feel him pulsing as he comes, burying himself deep inside me as he fills me. I'm addicted to his reaction, I want to make him come over and over again just so I can watch him.

We're both covered with a sheen of sweat as he collapses back into the chair, taking me with him and keeping me close. I really should attempt to clean up but neither of us care as we sit, wrapped up in each other, attempting to recover our breath between slow, sensual kisses.

"That was… Fuck," he says on a happy sigh.

"Yeah, yeah it was."

I can't think straight enough to come up with a better response than that.

"I wish I'd asked you this before, but, Harriet, will you go on a date with me tomorrow?"

I chuckle. "I'd love to."

CHAPTER TWENTY-SEVEN
Liam

"Good morning!" Katie calls, letting herself into my house as usual.

"Morning!" I shout from the kitchen and return to my task at hand. Packing a picnic.

Harriet left about an hour ago to change for our date. Between the extremely hot sex and sleeping, we didn't get around to talking about the logistics of our secret relationship, which is why I waited until she'd left to ring Katie and beg her to bring her picnic basket.

"What are you doing?" She looks over my shoulder at the pile of picnic items I've just unpacked from my early morning Sainsbury's run.

"What do you think I'm doing?"

"Making a mess," she deadpans. She isn't wrong.

Making herself at home, she helps herself to a coffee and takes a seat at the table while I search high and low for some sort of Tupperware.

She watches me carefully, sipping on her steaming hot cup as I take inventory of the food spread out across my kitchen bench.

Party sausages, check.

Mini sausage rolls, check.

Mini pork pies, check.

Scotch eggs, check.

"Is this too much pig?" I ask my cousin, looking from the pile of snacks to the ham for the sandwiches.

"Yes, that is without a doubt too much pig."

I pick up the wafer-thin ham and take it back to the fridge, swapping it for the cooked chicken instead.

"So, you're going on a picnic."

"Yeah."

"Judging by the amount of food you're packing, I assume you're taking someone?" She quirks an eyebrow over her mug.

"I'll tell you, but I need you to be discreet." I know she won't tell anyone, but I needed to say it out loud.

"You're going with Harriet."

"How do you know?"

"Because I just called around to drop off the jacket Jayne lent me last night, and in sneaks Harriet, looking all sheepish and smug doing her walk of shame."

My emotions betray me and a smile spreads right across my face.

"You hooked up, didn't you?" I expected her to be happy for us, but she's stoic.

"Yeah, and I know it's not a great idea. Both of us could get sacked if we're found out. But we've got a plan."

"That's not my issue here," she says, her tone heavy with disappointment.

"I thought you'd be happy for us."

"I am happy for you. I firmly believe that you two are made for each other and I'm relieved I don't need to watch you eye-fucking each other constantly if you're actually shagging."

I can sense a 'but' coming.

"Then what's wrong?"

"You still haven't told her about your dad, have you?"

Sighing, I flop down into the chair opposite. "No."

"You can't start a relationship without being a hundred per cent honest with her. Not only that, but Zach and I both know that you're keeping it from her. If she finds out another way, that makes us as bad as you. She's my friend, Liam."

"I know, it's just… I don't want to lose her. I promise, I'll tell her. I just need a bit of time to figure out what I'm going to say first, so I don't scare her away."

"Fine, but make sure you do it soon."

I'm relieved when she lets the issue drop. For now, at least.

She returns to her coffee in silence, and I return to making the sandwiches, packing them in the bag along with the selection of pig.

"Leave the scotch egg. Harriet doesn't like eggs," Katie says, jumping up on to the counter next to me, noticing the container I was about to put in the bag.

"Good save, thanks." I put them back in the fridge. "So now are you going to give me your gossip?" I prod her in the rib with my index finger and she laughs happily.

"Jayne and I are sort of dating," Katie says with a grin

169

spreading from ear to ear. "Although, I haven't actually asked her on a date yet. I should really do that, shouldn't I?"

"Yeah, you really should." I laugh as she hops down from the bench.

"Am I dismissed now, or do you need anything else?"

"Actually, yeah. Before you go, I wanted to speak to you about something."

Sensing the seriousness of my tone, she takes a seat back at the table.

"I've been thinking about selling this place. I think I need a change of scenery in my life."

She gives me a sad smile. Out of everyone, she knows how hard it's been to come to the conclusion that moving out of my childhood home, the one thing I have left connecting me to Mam, is the right thing to do.

"You'd probably get a decent amount for it, cottages on the ABC streets are in high demand, that one on Barnard Street sold for £135k and that was without the loft conversion. Where would you move to?"

"Maybe Seaburn. Somewhere close to the beach I think, with a bit of a garden. Detached if I can afford it, that way I don't have to hear my elderly neighbours going at it like rabbits every night."

"Gross." Katie shivers. "We could be neighbours again. Yay! It's been so long since we lived next door to each other."

"You know, maybe I'll look at Land's End, or John o'Groats, instead."

"Har-Har," she replies sarcastically before turning serious. "Where has this come from, anyway?"

"I've been thinking about life a bit lately. Maybe it's an existential crisis or something, but I've decided I'm not signing on for another season with Whitton, and figure a whole life upheaval is necessary." I heave out a sigh preparing myself. "I can't do this anymore, Katie. And before you jump to conclusions, I was thinking about doing this long before I met Harriet. If Mam could see me, she'd tell me to do what makes me happy, and this isn't it, so when my contract ends in a few months' time, I'm done."

"That's huge. What will you do?"

"I have no idea. I've got enough money saved to support me for at least a year. Maybe I'll try to get another theatre job, maybe I'll try something else instead. All I know is I need to get this place sorted out if I'm going to try and sell it."

"I'm so proud of you, you know." She comes to stand next to me, wrapping her arms around my shoulders from the side. "You deserve to be happy."

"You can go now," I say with a laugh. It felt so good to get how I feel off my chest and to know I have her support alongside Harriet's. I know I can do this and I won't be alone.

CHAPTER TWENTY-EIGHT
Liam

I pull up outside Harriet's house just before eleven. Jayne answers when I knock. She's grinning mischievously, obviously someone is feeling meddlesome this morning.

"Harriet, your boyfriend's here," she sings up the stairs without taking her eyes off me. "I don't have to do the whole, *murder you in your sleep* speech again, do I?" She crosses her arms and narrows her gaze at me.

"Nope, the message was loud and clear the last time, Jayne." I smile.

"What are your intentions with my sister?"

"What are your intentions with my cousin?"

"Touché, Mr Wright. Touché."

I nod smugly that I won that round.

"Jayne, leave him alone please," Harriet groans, coming down the stairs behind her sister. "God, you're so annoying."

She's wearing a short, printed romper. The various shades of green and blue making up the tropical pattern emphasises her tanned legs that appear to go on for days. The belt around her waist accentuates the curve of her hips and, fuck me, I'm staring at her boobs. Although it's a halter top and not a millimetre of cleavage is showing, I can't look away knowing exactly what's beneath that silky fabric.

"You look unreal." I lean in to kiss her.

"So do you."

"Tell me..." Jayne says with more mischief in her eyes. "Are you boyfriend and girlfriend now?"

"Yes," we both answer in unison, grinning at each other like teenagers. Even though we've not yet defined our relationship, it's good to know we're on the same page here.

"God you guys are going to be one of those couples, aren't you?" Jayne sighs, gagging dramatically. And here's me thinking Harriet was the actress of the family.

"Fuck off, Jayne," Harriet snaps.

"See ya!" her sister sings, satisfied with her mischief for today, skipping back upstairs.

"Ugh, sorry about that," Harriet apologises.

"There's nothing to apologise for, I had a visit from Katie this morning, so I've had it too."

She laughs. "I guess our secret relationship is secret other than Jayne and Katie... And also, my mam... I couldn't help myself. I was so happy when I came home all sexed up this morning by the man of my dreams."

She looks up at me from beneath her thick black lashes, knowing it's a sure fire way to get off the hook.

"Where are your parents?" I ask, noting the house is quiet.

"Dad is asleep, and Mam is visiting the hospice. He's

moving in on Friday, so I think she's signing paperwork and getting things sorted."

"Babe, I'm sorry." I pull her into my arms and rub her back, feeling some of the tension melt away beneath my palm.

"He needs it. He isn't sleeping much at night anymore, and neither is anyone else because we worry. At least if we know he's safe and looked after, we might rest easier."

"Have the doctors given you an update on his condition?"

"He's deteriorating quickly, he's got a month, maybe two." She snuggles further into my arms. "They can't be sure."

"If you'd rather stay here today, I understand. Our date can wait."

"No, I need to distract myself. The nurses have upped his painkillers this morning to try to give him a chance to rest, so he'll likely doze all day. Katie is going to come over and keep Jayne company anyway, so I doubt they want us hanging around cramping their style." She smiles at the mention of Katie and Jayne.

She picks up her light denim jacket and her handbag before shouting bye to her sister who responds with, "Don't be silly, wrap the willy."

"It's a bit late for that warning!" Harriet calls back.

"Ugh, gross!" Jayne responds, sounding a lot like my cousin and we both laugh.

When we climb into my car, I hand her the cable to plug her phone in and she picks the soundtrack.

Our destination for the day is Hamsterley Forest, a large 5000-acre Forest in County Durham. It's about an hour's drive.

Harriet's playlist is as expected: Taylor Swift, Miley Cyrus, Olivia Rodrigo and musical theatre, an odd mix of songs when it's on shuffle.

"Oh, I love this song." Harriet bounces up and down in her seat. "I think it might be my favourite from a musical."

The windows are down in the car, the wind blowing her hair back from her face. She looks gorgeous and as if it were possible, I think I fall for her a little bit more when she starts to sing along to "As Long As You're Mine" from *Wicked*.

Harriet would make a wonderful Elphaba; she could give Idina Menzel herself a run for her money, no doubt about that. She obviously isn't expecting me to jump in and sing along to Fiyero's verse, because her reaction is comical. She swings her entire body in her seat, her smile lighting up her face as she watches me. I take her hand as I keep my eyes on the road and sing to her. Not as Fiyero and Elphaba, but as us.

Although we've never sung together before, I mean, she didn't even know I could sing until a second ago, she still manages to harmonise with me perfectly when the characters come together to close the song.

When the song drifts to an end, she lets out a joyous scream from the passenger seat. I let out a loud laugh at her reaction because I hadn't planned to join in. I couldn't help myself and it felt amazing.

"I can't believe you can sing!" She slaps my arm. "Why didn't you tell me?"

"You didn't ask." I shrug, and she scoffs at my response.

"I didn't think you could get any more attractive but, shit, you're amazing." She fans herself dramatically.

"I haven't sung properly for years, at least, not in front of people. I usually reserve it for the shower. I would sing around the house with my mam and after she died, I couldn't face singing with someone else."

"Thank you for singing with me." She brings our joined hands to her lips, kissing my knuckles.

"I'll sing with you whenever you want. That was a lot of fun."

"Have you ever performed in front of an audience?"

"Never, I don't have the confidence."

"What other musicals do you know? Obviously, *Waitress* since it's your favourite… but what else?"

"I know all the words to *Hamilton*, so I guess that makes me a rapper too?"

For the rest of the journey, we perform a two person show of act one of *Hamilton* and don't stop smiling and laughing the entire time. If Harriet doesn't know the lyrics, she makes them up, calling it 'freestyling'. I also learn that she can't say the word 'phenomenon' which entertains me to no end.

"Okay, on the way home I say we do act two, what do you reckon?" Harriet asks when we pull into the car park and find a spot to park in a shaded area and out of the way of other cars.

"Sounds like a plan to me."

I have literally not stopped grinning since I picked her up and can't see myself stopping any time soon.

Looking around the carpark, I find a space quickly and swing in, pulling the handbrake on and switching off the engine.

"Oh," she says in surprise when I lean over to her side to kiss her, unable to keep my hands off her any longer. "Ohhhh..." she says again in understanding, jumping up onto her knees and wrapping her arms around my neck. She takes control, deepening her kiss by sliding her tongue in my mouth, my arousal becoming more and more noticeable. Like last night, the simple act of kissing her has me hard and panting with need.

We get a little carried away for a moment, trying to navigate our bodies around the gearstick and handbrake of my car so we can get closer to one another. Obviously, it doesn't work, so we make do with letting our hands explore one another as we make out. I can't get enough of how soft and smooth her skin is. When I draw my lips down her neck, she lets out a gasp of delight and I think it might be my new favourite sound.

Our movements are frantic and desperate when I bring my lips back to hers, my hand skirting across the hard bud of her nipple. I love exploring what makes her release those sexy little whimpers and moans, and this seems to be a favourite of hers.

I'm having a tough time remembering why we aren't at home right now.

When our hands start to wander too much, mine pushing up the short leg of her romper and caressing the smooth skin of her bum and hers palming my erection over my shorts as I strain against them. I vaguely become aware that we're in a public car park, so I pull back slightly. She looks at me with dazed eyes and sticks out her bottom lip in a display of protest. It's a little swollen from where I just nibbled on it, so I kiss her again softly. I rest my forehead against hers as we regain control of our breathing.

"We should get out of this car before we lose control again." I rub my nose along hers, desperate to kiss her again.

"Yeah, it's probably for the best."

We tear ourselves apart and sit back in our own seats. Harriet lowers the sun visor to neaten up her hair in the mirror, and I glare down at my crotch because I can't step out of the car like this. She laughs as I squint my eyes into the distance, doing my best to think of unsexy things.

CHAPTER TWENTY-NINE
Harriet

"The picnic basket is a really cute touch," I tell Liam. Just like his, my smile hasn't left my face since he picked me up this morning. Come to think of it, I don't think I've stopped smiling since he kissed me for the first time yesterday afternoon.

We're floating on cloud nine and I'm grateful we have the week off to explore this romance blossoming between us without the added pressure of Diane.

"I'm glad you appreciate it, I think it rather suits me." He swings it by his side with a skip. "There's a nice spot, along the end of the trail. It's usually quite quiet away from the crowds, so I thought we could make our way along there?"

"That sounds perfect. Lead the way."

He holds out his hand and I take it, weaving my fingers through his. It's so exciting to be walking around in public holding hands as though this is perfectly normal and what we're doing isn't a huge risk to our livelihoods.

Walking along the path following the Bedburn Beck, we pass huge climbing frames and Viking-inspired playground apparatus made from wood and other natural materials. We come to an empty course of ropes, chains and stumps designed to test balance. Handing me the picnic basket, Liam is the first to jump up to attempt it. He does a good job, making it to the end without falling once, unlike me who falls off the very first log. Liam jogs back towards me to take my hand to help me along while carrying the basket in the other.

We make it a little way along the trail before a young girl, she can't be older than eighteen, stops us.

"Excuse me," she says nervously, looking back to her friends who give an encouraging nod. "Are you Harriet and Liam?"

"Yeah." I glance at Liam to see if he recognises this girl.

"Omg I love your TikToks. I wish you'd do more together!"

Over the course of the past four weeks, Liam has briefly appeared in a number of TikTok videos and live Instagram streams, usually he's in the background or offering techie advice. Although they do prove to be the most popular with my followers, I never thought we'd get recognised in public because of them.

"Oh, wow, thanks. I think we should do more together too, but this one's a little camera shy." I point my thumb towards Liam.

"I really like your technical videos too. I want to do what you do when I graduate," she says to Liam.

"You want to be a techie?" His eyebrows shoot up in surprise.

"Yeah, I go to Sixth Street Theatre School. I want to be a stage manager."

"I went to Sixth street too, and Harriet did only a few years after me."

"Wow, seriously?" We both nod and the girl looks over her shoulder at her friends who amble closer to us. "We all go there. My friends are actors, they're really good."

"In that case, I look forward to seeing your names on some big productions in the future," Liam says encouragingly, and the girls collectively swoon. I don't blame them, because seeing the way he inspires these young girls has me swooning too.

After taking a few selfies with them, we say goodbye and continue our walk along the beck.

"That was insane, right?" I say as we walk away hand in hand along the stream, the water babbling gently beside us. "I've been recognised before but only ever in a theatre environment, never randomly in public."

"Yeah, it was definitely weird!"

"The fans have spoken. They want you in another video." I nudge him with my shoulder.

"I might be persuaded to join you in a few." He stops walking. Still holding my hand, he pulls me in closer and caresses my face. "I might even sing with you, but I'd have to get you to give me a few lessons first, so I don't totally embarrass myself."

"You have nothing to be embarrassed about, you're amazing. If you really need to, I can show you how to neaten up your performance, but really, your natural voice is perfect the way it is. I for one find it a huge turn on," I say, my voice low and seductive.

"Is that so?" He lowers his face slowly to mine, drawing out the anticipation of his kiss.

"Mhmm." I nod and finally he brushes his lips against mine.

I could kiss this man all day, no doubt about it.

"Why don't we have a nice romantic picnic now and then later, I can serenade you at my place?"

"Let's get this picnic on the road, what are we waiting for?" I start to speed walk, tugging on his arm, and he laughs heartily.

A few minutes later, we reach a large picnic area. It's busy and packed with families, which is weird since Liam said the spot was private enough for us to fool around in.

"Keep going," he instructs as I look at him in confusion. A little further along the trail we come to a small wooden bridge leading to the other side of the beck. The bridge is narrow, and we have to cross single file, so Liam leads the way.

At the other side we take the steep gravel path leading up through the trees, deeper into the woods. Beneath the close canopy of the lush green conifers that tower above us, the sounds of the families we passed only moments ago fade away into silence making way for the sounds of the forest to come alive. The path we're walking along must follow the stream because although I can't see the water, I can hear it along with the rustling of the leaves above us and some crickets chirping in the brush out of sight.

We come to another wide-open space to our left, a fenced off meadow by the looks of it, which is bathed in sunlight, but Liam veers off to the left instead.

The path is covered by undergrowth and looks to have been formed by footprints instead of machinery like the other trails, but it's definitely there. He ducks under a low hanging branch, then holds it up so I don't have to bend as low and offers me his hand so we can clamber down the rocky outcrop until we get to a flat pebbly area by the stream.

"This is amazing," I say, taking in my surroundings. Liam wasn't wrong when he said this was private. We're hidden on all sides, although there is space in the canopy to allow the sunlight to penetrate to the forest floor.

There is life everywhere. From the moss growing on the trees, and the wildflowers growing in the land untouched by humans, to the little beetles I spotted on the rocks coming down here.

"It's beautiful, isn't it?"

I watch him intently while he works in a methodical silence spreading out our feast between us on a tartan picnic blanket.

"This looks delicious." I marvel at the thought he's put into planning this.

"There's not too much pig, is there?"

"I did wonder what that cryptic text from Katie was about this morning, but no, this is the perfect amount of pig."

"Text?"

I try to hold in my laughter as I open my phone to read it to him. "Compliment the pig, he's self-conscious."

"I'm going to kill her." He feigns annoyance until his laughter breaks through. "Well, the pig is ready so dig in."

"Okay, I've got one. It's pork related too so buckle up," Liam says as we lie on the blanket together, long finished our picnic but neither ready to leave our tranquil spot. I'm tucked into his side with his arm below my head like a pillow. "Would you rather have sausages for fingers or toes?"

We've been playing would you rather for twenty minutes and, so far, we've agreed that we'd rather fight a badger than a kangaroo since they're smaller and probably easier to restrain, and that we'd rather have long arms like Mr Tickle than short ones like a T-rex because, you know, hugs.

The last one resulted in a lengthy conversation about why T-rexes are so grumpy, and it always came back to the fact that they can't hug properly.

"What would happen if I ate the sausages on my fingers? Would they grow back?" I ask.

"Uh, Yeah, sure. Why not."

"What kind of sausage? Like a fancy schmancy Cumberland or a bog-standard hotdog?"

"Whatever you want."

"The best sausage I've ever tasted I bought from Beamish Hall Christmas Market. I went with my mam and Auntie Tricia one year and spent thirty quid on sausages. It was amazing. They were salted caramel flavoured and honestly, I can still taste them now."

"Salted caramel sausage?" He pulls a face.

"Hey, don't knock it, they tasted unreal! I just can't remember the name of the company that made them, so I've not had them since… Okay, I'd have sausages for fingers, easy access for snacking, you know."

"Good logic."

"Although…" I add, not quite convinced myself.

"Go on."

"If I ate them all the time, I'd get sick of them and then I'd have ruined my favourite sausage."

"So, sausages for toes?"

"Yeah, sausages for toes, final answer." I sigh. "My turn. Would you rather everyone around you be able to hear your thoughts or for everyone to have access to your internet history?"

"Oh easy, internet history."

"Really?" I crane my neck to look up at him, quirking a suggestive eyebrow.

"Yeah, because my internet history is squeaky clean, but since I've met you my thoughts are constantly indecent."

"Liam Wright, is that so?" I throw myself on top of him, leaning down with a hand either side of his head.

In a low gravelly voice, he replies, "Do you want me to remind you?"

"Oh, fuck me. Quite literally, please."

He pulls me to him with his hand on my neck and kisses me hungrily. He flips me onto my back taking control and, Christ, he feels incredible on top of me. The weight of his thigh pressing between my legs provides a slight relief to the ache that has resided there all day, but it's not enough.

He moans into my hair as I move my lips to his neck and

up to his ear, grazing his skin with my teeth. I let my hands move down his back and pull him closer to me so he rubs against my hip. I can feel him stiffen through our clothes as he lets out another tortured sound of pleasure before kissing me again.

"Fuck, why didn't I wear something with easier access?" I groan out loud in frustration when his hand travels up my thigh below the shorts of my playsuit and gets stuck before he's able to make contact where I need him most. This outfit is not ideal for a woodland romp and we both know it.

"Shall we go home?" Liam asks breathlessly.

"Yeah, let's go."

He kisses me one last time before we both jump up. Together we hastily pack up our blanket and picnic basket and make a swift exit back to the car.

CHAPTER THIRTY
Harriet

"Oh, my fuck!" Liam says on a long breath as he flops back on the bed next to me, having given me not one but two incredible orgasms, one after the other.

"You can say that again." Both of us breathe heavily as I gaze across at him looking so comfortable in my bed like he belongs right here.

It's only been two days since we were last together after our woodland date, but I clearly have zero chill, because the second he walked through the door I was ushering him straight to my bed, explaining we had a free house for a few hours and need to make the most of it. After that, our clothes might as well have disintegrated, because he had us both naked and was going down on me in a flash as he told me how much he missed me.

He lets out a happy little groan as he rests his hand behind his head and gestures for me to snuggle in.

"One sec." I give him a quick peck on the cheek. Tugging on his discarded t-shirt that now belongs to me, I run to the bathroom to clean up. When I'm done, the t-shirt comes off again and I climb back into bed to snuggle into my favourite spot in the crook of his armpit, resting my head on his bicep.

I let out a sigh of sheer, unadulterated bliss.

"Back where I belong," I say, and he chuckles as I nuzzle in. I close my eyes and inhale the side of his neck, his usual rough manly scent mixed with sex is my absolute favourite thing in the world.

"How are you doing, babe?"

I've been in constant contact with him while I've been caring for Dad over the past couple of days, but I appreciate him asking me again, even more so because I know it's hard for him too, watching what happened to him and his mam happen to another undeserving family.

"I'm exhausted," I admit. "Physically and emotionally."

"I'm so proud of you. It's not easy caring for someone who's sick."

"Thanks, I don't know how Jayne and Mam have done it all this time with no help. I've had the Macmillan nurses coming in to help me and it's still been hard."

"Where is everyone today? I assume not here since, well, you know." He waves his hands over our naked bodies entwined under a thin sheet in my double bed, the bright pink bedspread I had as a teenager in a bundle on the floor where we tossed it.

When I moved home from London, Mam decorated my old room back the way it was when I left, pink and white walls minus the *Twilight* and *Hunger Games* film posters. My white wrought-iron bed and a little wooden desk in the corner. You'd never guess this room had been a home gym for the time I moved away.

After all the crap I'd endured in London, it was comforting to return to my childhood room; it made me feel safe again.

"Jayne is out with Katie, and Dad wanted to take Mam out on a date. He dressed up all smart. It was so cute. Me and Jayne helped him pick out a nice shirt and his nurse arranged to take him in his chair down to Seaham so they could share fish and chips by the statue of Tommy. He's gone off solid food now, but it's something they used to do a lot before he got sick."

"That's really romantic."

"It's Dad all over. He's so over the top romantic, it's adorable and sets a high bar when it comes to relationships. He wants to get a takeaway tonight with all of us, Katie too, if you'd like to join my crazy family? Be warned though, Dad talks about you all the time, since you made it possible for him to come watch me perform. I swear he has such a man crush on you."

"I just want to make his little girl happy. And I'd love to stop and eat with you all."

"And that you do." I lean up and kiss him softly.

"I'll remember that night for as long as I live. The look on your face as you spotted him was one of pure joy. And then, when you came off the stage and everyone was crying, it was torture because I wanted to be the one to comfort you. I wanted to be the first to wrap my arms around you and hold you, but I couldn't. I stood back and waited my turn."

"It's our turn now, Liam Wright," I say softly, caressing his face and bringing my lips to his once again.

"And you are well worth the wait, Harriet Adams."

CHAPTER THIRTY-ONE
Liam

Harriet's dad, Dean, is in good spirits when he comes into the living room a few hours after returning home. He's walking with the help of his Macmillan nurse and although he hides it well, there's a small wince of pain when he sits down. No one acknowledges it and I know from experience they'll be protecting his dignity as much as they can.

Cancer doesn't discriminate and it also doesn't allow for a dignified end.

"Liam, it's good to see you again, son." He smiles at me fondly. "I see you finally built up the courage to ask my daughter out."

"Daaaad." Harriet groans.

"It's good to see you too." I laugh. "And yes, I did. I wish I'd done it earlier."

"I assume she's been keeping you on your toes the past few weeks. She's a feisty one, but sensitive too." He chuckles and flicks his thumb towards his eldest daughter. Their banter warms me inside while simultaneously making me wish I had a dad like Dean Adams.

"You could say that."

Harriet's eyes widen, though she laughs and slaps my arm playfully. "Oi! You're meant to be on my side."

"Unlike this one," he says as Jayne enters the room, "she was always the feral one, getting in trouble for starting fights with the boys."

"I finished them too," Jayne says proudly, "still do." She narrows her eyes at me, before breaking and laughing. "Harriet, Mam wants you in the kitchen."

"Okay." She glances between me and her dad. "No ganging up on me while I'm not in the room. I'm watching you both." She brings her fingers to her eyes and wags them between us.

"I actually wanted to talk to you." Dean glances at the door to make sure we're not overheard.

"Okay," I say nervously as his face turns serious.

"Thank you again for what you did to get me to that show. You made me and my family very happy that night, and judging by the smile that's been plastered on my daughter's face since she met you, you make her happy too."

"That's all I want, to see her smile." It's my turn to glance at the door this time. Clearing my throat, I continue, "I love your daughter. I know it's fast, but I know she's the one for me and one day, in the future, of course, I'd like to ask her to marry me."

Dean watches me, searching my eyes. It's fast, but I want to do the right thing and be honest about what my intentions are. I have a lot to talk to her about when it comes to my own dad, and I will, but for now, I'm focusing on us.

"It must seem fast and it probably is, but—"

"Son," he interrupts, his voice even. "I had known Shelley two weeks before I proposed to her. A week after that we were standing in front of that iconic anvil, getting married at Gretna Green."

"Wow," I say, not knowing what else to say.

"If you say she's the one and she feels the same, then you do things at your speed. And if you love my daughter and promise you'll spend your life making her happy, then that's enough for me. You have my blessing."

"Thank you, it really means a lot. And I promise I'll look after her, and Jayne for that matter."

"Thank you," he says, just as Harriet enters the room with a glass of blackcurrant squash that she places on the side table for him.

"Getting along nicely I see." She sits on the arm of the chair next to me. "Talking about your favourite girl?"

"Talking about you not to you." Dean sticks his tongue out at her.

Dean and I exchange a knowing look and smile at one another, safe in the knowledge that our conversation will be kept safe until the time comes.

CHAPTER THIRTY-TWO
Liam

Friday rolls around quickly. It's a day Harriet has been dreading, which means I've been on edge all day not having heard from her since the first thing this morning.

She texted me when they were on the way to drop her dad off at the hospice, but I've heard nothing since and it's now well after eight p.m. I know I should relax. It's a huge day for her family and I'm sure she's leaning on them for support.

Picking up my phone for the umpteenth time today, there's still nothing. I can't help the niggling in my stomach that something might be wrong.

My fears multiply tenfold when Jayne's name lights up my Fitbit screen with an incoming call on my phone. Jayne has never called me. I only have her number in case of emergencies.

I dive over my bed, scrambling helplessly to the opposite side where my phone sits on charge on the bedside table.

"Jayne?"

"Can you come over?" Her voice is weary as if she has been crying, which is a stupid observation because, yeah, it's been a sad day. "Harriet has fallen apart, and I don't know how to help. We got home a few hours ago, and she's refused to eat anything and has locked herself in her room. I can hear her crying. She doesn't want to talk to us, but I thought maybe she'd talk to you. Or at the very least let you in."

"I'll be right there," I tell her and hang up. I run around my room like a man on a mission, shoving things haphazardly into an overnight bag because there is no way in hell I'm leaving her alone when she feels like this. I knew something was wrong. I should have insisted that I wait there for her coming home.

My last stop before I bolt out the door is the fridge to pick up the gift I bought for her, and then I'm on my way.

The roads are empty, and I thank my lucky stars that I hit every green light on my route from High Barnes to Ashbrooke, so I'm parking on her drive in a matter of minutes.

Jayne must have been watching for me coming and has the door open ready for me to dash straight up the stairs, taking them two at a time, to Harriet's bedroom.

I knock and there's no answer. Jayne joins her mam at the other end of the landing outside of her own bedroom, hugging her arms tightly over her chest.

"Harriet?" I call through the door. "Can you let me in?"

The lock clicks open and a heartbroken Harriet appears in a crack in the door. Her eyes are red, and her cheeks tear stained. My heart breaks for her and it takes all I've got not to break down with her.

"Babe," I say softly, and she pulls the door open wider, diving into my open arms. I walk her back into her room as fresh tears spill out of her pretty eyes and saturate my t-shirt. I sit on the edge of her bed and pull her into my lap, holding her close and doing my best at being soothing.

I want to cry with her as the memories of eighteen-year-old me come flooding back, but now isn't the time, she needs me to be strong. The other Adams women watch helplessly as Harriet falls apart. I give them a reassuring nod that I've got this, and they leave us alone, closing the door to Harriet's room behind them.

I kick off my shoes and shift back up the bed, not letting go of her as I move us both into a more comfortable position, lying on her pillows next to her.

"Do you want to talk about it?" I feel the definite shake of her head. "That's okay, we'll just lie like this."

Slowly her violent sobs calm until they trail off altogether. When she lets out a little snore, I realise she's cried herself to sleep. I rearrange her on the bed so she's in a comfortable position and make my way downstairs to get her a drink.

"Is she okay?" her mam asks when I enter the kitchen. It's been a gruelling day for everyone, and it's clear to see the exhaustion in Shelley's shallow features.

"She cried herself to sleep. I wanted to bring these down and put them in the fridge." I hold the little white carrier bag out and her mam takes it off me. When she looks inside, her eyes warm with the memory and she nods before putting it in the fridge.

"Do you mind if I stay with her tonight?" I ask Shelley.

"Oh, bless you, you don't need to ask for permission, you're welcome any time."

I thank her. "What happened today? I haven't heard from

her since this morning."

"It finally hit her that Dean isn't going to come back here." Shelley's eyes fill up, as do Jayne's who is sitting curled up into a ball at the kitchen table. "She's a sensitive soul even though she tries to be tough, and I don't think she lets herself think about it."

I remember taking my mam to the same hospice as clearly as if it were yesterday. The moment she got settled into her bed, she looked comfortable and at peace. For the first time since she got sick, she had colour in her cheeks and her eyes didn't look as hollow as they did when she was in hospital. That's how I knew her death was imminent and she wouldn't be coming home.

Shelley pours two glasses of water, and I tell her and Jayne that I'm here for all of them, no matter what they need.

When I go back upstairs, I place our drinks down on each of her bedside tables, plug her lifeless phone into charge and change into my checked pyjamas bottoms ready for bed.

Harriet may be sleeping but she looks anything but peaceful. Her face is still contorted with anguish, and I wish more than anything that I could take away her pain. I wish that if I erased that little line puckered between her eyebrows it would make things easier for her.

Turning off the big light, I climb into bed next to her, pulling her close so her back is pressed against my chest. She breathes out a soft whimper as I wrap my arms around her, shushing her, and just like that, her face relaxes as she melts into me.

I lie there for a while, my thoughts running wild in my head, listening to her breathe, and doing my best to comfort her through her bad dreams until eventually I fall asleep too.

CHAPTER THIRTY-THREE
Harriet

Blinding sunlight streams through the gap in my blinds and I throw my forearm over my eyes.

A soft snore comes from beside me and I turn in his embrace to find my boyfriend lying with his arms wrapped protectively around me, looking like a *GQ* model. Like, seriously, who looks this good when they're asleep? After hours of crying yesterday, I don't dare look in the mirror at what state I am in.

Sitting up, I see a glass of water and my phone on charge by my bed. Liam must have plugged it in for me because I know I didn't; I wasn't even capable of stringing together any words when I got home.

Very carefully, I extract myself from the safe cocoon of Liam's embrace and climb out of bed so I can tiptoe to the bathroom. When I'm done, I risk a glance in the mirror. My eyes are red and puffy, my lips swollen from all the crying.

I watch Liam fondly from my doorway for a brief moment, and when I get back into bed he stirs.

"Hey," he says, his eyes still half shut and his voice groggy. "What time is it?"

"Sorry, go back to sleep. I didn't mean to wake you. It's just after six."

Sleepily, he opens his arms wide and I curl up against his warm chest. Stroking my palms down his pecs, I revel in the feel of his muscles and the soft sprinkling of hair.

"How are you feeling?" he asks.

"Sad." That's exactly how I feel. Sad and numb.

"That's okay, we don't have to get out of bed today if you don't want to. And if you do want to, we can drive and see your dad."

"Thank you." I caress his face and press my lips to his. "Thank you for being exactly what I need."

"You can always depend on me, Harriet."

When we wake up again a few hours later, this time, I'm the big spoon with my arms straining to make it all the way around Liam's broad chest.

"I don't care what anyone says, I love being the little spoon," Liam says, making me chuckle, something I didn't think would be possible twelve hours ago. "I could get used to waking up like this." He rubs his hands over my forearms and links his fingers with mine.

"Me too."

"Oh!" He suddenly springs to life. "I brought you a present." He jumps out of bed far too eagerly for having just woken up.

"Ignore that, he's excited to wake up with you too," he says looking down at the tent in his plaid pyjama bottoms. He does that thing where he concentrates at a point in the distance as he tries to get rid of his hard-on. I can think of another way to take care of it, but he bats my hand away when I reach for him.

"I want to give you your present first."

As soon as he is decent – I mean not sporting a massive erection – we make our way into the kitchen. He opens the fridge and confusion settles over me when he hands me a white plastic bag.

Peering inside, I stand frozen for a while, processing the gift.

Salted caramel sausages from The Northumbrian Sausage Company.

"How?" I ask, my voice barely more than a whisper.

"I spent a few hours on the internet searching for traders of Beamish Hall Christmas Market over the past few years, and I found them," he says as though this isn't a big deal. And maybe it wouldn't be to most people. I dare say getting a pack of sausages from your boyfriend might come across as a little bit weird. But, to me, this means the world.

This means so much more than a packet of sausages.

I mentioned them one time and he listened. He remembered that ridiculous conversation about how I would rather have sausages for toes than fingers. He remembered my elaborate explanation as to why. And not only did he remember, but he took the very little information I had given him and spent hours trying to find them knowing how happy it would make me.

"I can't believe you did this for me." I look from him to the sausages and back again until my eyes blur with more tears.

"Are they the right ones? I can go back and—"

I launch myself at him, cutting off his words by kissing him through my huge wet tears.

"I need you to tell me if these are good or bad tears." His arms are tight around my waist supporting me.

"I love you, Liam," I tell him for the first time. My heart feels like it might burst.

"I love you too, Harriet."

CHAPTER THIRTY-FOUR
Liam

I could get used to waking up next to Harriet. I don't even mind that every time I breathe in, I inhale a chunk of her hair, which I've come to discover is absolutely wild in the morning.

In fact, I love waking up with Harriet's hair in my airways, because she looks so completely gorgeous it's worth the hairball.

"Do you have time for breakfast before you go see your dad?" I ask as I eventually drag myself away from her lips on Monday morning. After two nights staying at her house, we stayed at mine last night. "My call isn't until eleven at the theatre."

"Yeah, I have loads of time. I'm going to the hospice for eleven too, so I have a few hours."

We visited her dad together on Saturday and then again yesterday. It was fun, and I think it helped Harriet to see him comfortable for the first time in a while. In the moments her dad was awake, the three of us played chess, me and Harriet against her dad. Of course, we lost because neither of us have played chess in our lives.

Having only met Harriet's dad a handful of times, it

surprised me how easily he welcomed me into his family. He calls me son as though I'm part of the family already. It kills me knowing that if we had more time together, he'd become much more of a dad to me than my actual father. In fact, he already might be.

"Are you going to kick his arse in chess?" I ask.

"No matter how much we practice I don't think we'll ever win." She sighs. A sombre expression passes over her features as we silently acknowledge that we don't have enough time left with him to come anywhere close to beating him.

It's so unfair that a man like him should be taken too early. He's a good man who would do anything for his family, and he gets taken in such a cruel way just like Mam.

Harriet says he's been talking a lot about his funeral lately. He's had a hand in planning it, which she hates as she's still pretending he's got time left, but it's inevitable and it makes him feel more in control.

Each day that passes, he declines more and although he's coping better in the hospice, I know it's not going to save him, so if he finds comfort in being prepared then so be it.

"I don't think I'm ready to get out of bed yet," Harriet says. "I want to stay in this dream land forever."

We've both been dreading today because we're about to burst our lovers' bubble and head back to the real world. While we're at work we need to go back to what it was before, avoiding being alone and pretending we aren't madly in love with each other.

"Life can wait another few hours." I lean down to kiss her hungrily as if I haven't been kissing her since we walked through my door last night.

"What about breakfast?" she asks breathily as I stroke my fingers between her legs.

God, I love it when she wears nothing but my t-shirt.

"I'm hungry for a different kind of breakfast." I tease her entrance with the tip of my middle finger. She gets the hint and kisses me hard.

I toy and tease her entrance until she's bucking against my hand desperate for more. When I disappear under the quilt, she tangles her fingers in my hair, her nails grazing against my scalp, sending sparks of sheer desire right to my dick.

When I have the first taste of her, I feel like an addict getting a hit. I growl in pleasure because as usual she tastes so good and one lick is nowhere near enough. I'm so attuned to her body that I know exactly what elicits a moan and a gasp. I know she's close when my name flies from her lips like an expletive.

Her body tenses, her back arches and her feet dig into my back; she's so close I can feel her tightening around my fingers.

"Oh god! Oh, Liam! Yes! Yes!" She comes apart quickly on my hand, her walls clamping down on me as she cries out repeatedly.

I don't immediately pull back, instead I lick her slowly and softly until her ragged breathing evens out and she lets go of her vice-like grip on my hair.

"Fuck, I'm sorry," she says, smoothing down the tufts that are sticking up and I laugh. "I tried to last longer but I couldn't."

"There's plenty of time," I say, keeping my voice low. "I'm

just getting started."

After a long deliberation (not long at all), we decide it'd be best if we shower together, to save the planet and conserve water and protect the turtles or something as equally important.

It has to be the best idea I've ever had though, because the second we step under the hot and steamy stream of water, Harriet is wet and dropping to her knees in front of me.

"Holy fucking shit," I breathe, her blue-green eyes look up at me from beneath her thick lashes. Water is running down her perfect breasts and dripping off her nipples. She looks like every guy's fantasy, except, for some reason, I'm lucky enough for this to be real.

She closes her delicate fingers in a firm fist around my painfully hard dick, still aching from when I went down on her a few minutes ago. My entire body is tense, waiting in anticipation for the first contact from her plump wet lips. She gives me a wicked smile – guess she's showing me how it feels when I tease her.

I push her hair away from her face, holding it in my fist so I can see her better.

"You're so beautiful."

She strokes me slowly, as she watches a drop of moisture form on my tip. Without warning her tongue swipes it away and I damn near pass out from the contact.

My breathing is hoarse and erratic, as she teases me, licking me from base to tip but not taking me into her mouth.

I'm desperate so when she licks her full lips and seals them around the head of my dick unexpectedly, I let out a tortured moan. A second later, when she sucks me and pulls me as deep into the back of her throat as she can, every part of my nervous system crackles before bursting into flames. Heat spreads over my body and I'm worried that this time it's me that won't last.

I keep my gaze on her, watching her as she works me over, pushing me closer and closer to oblivion. When her free hand disappears between her legs, she lets out a soft moan that sends shivers from my dick right up my spine. My release is imminent. I'm desperate to come, but not like this, I want to be inside of her.

"Harriet, let me fuck you."

She removes her mouth from me and pauses all movements.

"Am I not doing it right?" A moment of insecurity flutters over her gorgeous features.

"This is the best blow job I've ever had, but, babe, I need to fuck you. Please?"

"I didn't think begging was a thing for me but hearing you beg might be my newest kink." She laughs sexily. Her naughty smile is back where it belongs.

She stands and turns to face the tiled walls, placing her palms flat against it to keep her steady as she looks at me over her shoulder, her eyes wide and innocent even though I know my girl is anything but.

When I slide my fingers against her from behind, I find her wet and ready for me. She moans as I tweak her nipple with one hand, and she easily takes a finger deep inside of her from my other.

The second my dick enters her it'll be game over for me; I need to get her as close as possible.

Letting go of her hard nipple, I reach my hand down over her stomach and find her swollen clit as I continue to stroke her from the inside. She's writhing against me, both of my hands pushing her to breaking point until she's crying out that she's close.

"Fuck me, Liam."

I sink into her tight wet heat slowly from behind before pulling out and back in again, going deeper and deeper until I'm fully sheathed by her, her body stretching to take all of me.

I pick up the pace as she begs me to fuck her harder, the sounds of our heavy breathing and wet skin slapping together beneath the steady stream of the shower.

"Babe! I'm not going to last here."

"Yes, right there!" She screams out my name over and over again as she shatters, clenching down around me. My toes curl, every muscle I possess tenses, my balls tighten and I explode inside her with a loud, guttural roar.

Her body goes limp in my arms as she loses control of her shaking legs, so I take her weight, supporting her as she continues to milk me with her climax, drawing out deep groans of sheer pleasure from deep within me as I empty everything I have into her.

"Babe, are you okay?" I chuckle affectionately at her dazed expression.

"Not to be dramatic, but that just changed my life."

CHAPTER THIRTY-FIVE
Liam

There's something incredible about having mind-blowing sex with the woman you love right before work that sets you up nicely for the day.

Four crew members come up to me by the end of my first hour to ask why I'm in such a great mood. I tell them I'm well rested from the break. Obviously, I can't tell them the real reason I'm so happy, but clearly being in an exciting new relationship is doing wonders for my personality.

"How was your week off?" Diane asks me as I'm organising the props ready to re-open the show tonight. The scenery is back in place after its repairs and it looks like we've never been away.

"It was fine. Quiet," I answer, not bothering to look up from the prop cabinet as I continue.

I haven't spoken to Di since she interrupted me and Harriet before the break, which is definitely out of character for us, but I've come to the realisation that I don't really care anymore.

"I met with your dad."

I immediately drop what I'm doing. "And what did he say?"

"Liam…" I'd recognise that tone anywhere. She's about to give me bad news. "Shall we sit down?" she asks.

"Just tell me."

"He doesn't think you're ready, Liam. He wants you to have a little more experience before he promotes you."

Her words cut me deeply. More experience? How on earth can I get more experience if he won't let me grow or work outside of the company? The contract he drew up for me traps me completely; there's no way out of it other than quitting.

Deep down, I knew that was the case.

I knew I'd have to quit to escape his hold on me. But quitting would also mean being apart from Harriet as the production leaves Sunderland and goes on tour, and I don't think I can do that either. At least if I stay, we can be close to each other, even if it means hiding away in secret.

"Did he ask about me?" I ask, catching her off guard.

"In what way?"

"In any way. Did he bring up my name in any capacity without being prompted by you?" I already know the answer by looking at her blank expression.

"Your dad loves you, Liam. I love you, you're as much of a son to me too. Your dad is an idiot, and he knows it. He just… he just doesn't know how to relate to you, which is why he makes these choices. Let me talk to him again."

I take a deep breath, steadying my nerves and burying all my emotional rage deep inside.

I smile the best fake smile I can muster. "Fine."

I know talking to Di isn't going to fix anything. I need to go directly to him, but she's his gatekeeper and I'll never get past her if she thinks I plan on doing that.

"Fine?"

"Yeah. If that's the way it has to be, then that's fine by me. I don't want to argue about it. I'm going to finish this and head out for some lunch for a little while," I add, hoping she'll get the hint and leave.

"Right, well. I'm glad we got that sorted."

I offer her a small smile and a nod.

Harriet

Liam knocks on my dressing room door at lunchtime not long after I arrive at the theatre for the rest of the day.

He looks around to make sure we're safe before entering the room. I close the door behind him and lock it.

When he sits on the chaise lounge, he lets out a loaded sigh.

"What's going on? What's wrong?" I'm worried now at the shift in his mood since this morning.

Standing again he pulls me to him, closing the distance between us completely, and kisses me hard. His hand placed possessively on the base of my spine sends sparks of desire racing all over my body. His apparent stress and anger fade away with each brush of our tongues. Wrapping my arms around his neck, I hoist myself up and entwine my legs around his waist without breaking from our passionate embrace.

He pulls away looking for a hard surface and spots my dressing table. In the sexiest move known to humankind, he takes my weight with one arm and swipes everything over to make room for me with the other. Usually, I'd be fuming if someone messed with my organisation and potentially smashed my pristine make-up palettes, but I'm so turned on right now I couldn't give a fuck.

My hands claw at his back and his neck, pulling him to me with my leg that's now wrapped around the back of his thigh. As I desperately grind against him, the only thing separating us is our clothes as he presses his erection into me, keeping me in position with his hands on my waist and thigh. The contact is almost enough to send me over the edge right here.

I whimper his name into his mouth when he runs his thumb over my nipple that strains through the thin fabric of my sports bra. He lets out a low groan in response.

"You're soaked, babe," he says gruffly as he rubs me through my leggings, and I gasp. "Is this for me?"

I nod and cry out as he increases pressure. I swear, I could come from this alone despite the countless orgasms he's given me daily since we got together.

When I undo his cargo pants to free him, I'm startled when Diane's voice echoes from the radio on his hip, calling his name like she always does when she senses he's up to no good with me. He stops kissing me, but we don't move apart. He rests his forehead on mine and we try to regain some control over ourselves. When he's able to speak without panting, he brings his radio to his mouth and speaks.

"On my way," he says before doing up his trousers and clipping it back in place.

"Liam, what's wrong?" I ask now my judgement isn't clouded by the lusty haze he inflicted on me.

"It's nothing, I have to go visit my dad that's all," he says without really explaining anything.

"Has something happened? I can come with you. When do you need to go?"

"I don't know yet, but don't worry about it, I don't need you to come. Everything is fine. I'm handling it."

"Liam—"

"Harriet, I said I'm handling it!" He recoils at his own words. "I'm sorry, babe. I'm stressed out and I just need to see him and sort everything out once and for all."

"It's okay." I take his hand.

"When I've spoken to him, I'll tell you everything. Please just trust that things will be okay."

"I trust you," I say, although I'm not sure exactly what he's asking me to trust him for.

He leans down and kisses me softly and slowly, breathing me in as though it's giving him life. This time, when he pulls back, our eyes meet and the air around us fills with so much love and tenderness.

"I love you, Harriet," he says with a regretful smile.

"I love you too."

Diane squawks his name down the radio again.

"You should go before she comes looking for you," I say, even though I'd give anything to keep him safe with me in this room right now.

CHAPTER THIRTY-SIX
Liam

Dad's office is slap bang in the middle of Leicester Square, a stone's throw from the famous Odeon cinema. It's prime theatre real estate around here, and I have to say, Whitton Production's head office is a little underwhelming.

I don't know what I expected, glitz and glamour maybe?

The entrance to the old building is a nondescript heavy wooden door; it could be anything. No signs lit up around it, nothing to say that the man I've spent my life trying to impress sits somewhere inside, which strikes me as odd when he loves attention from strangers.

As I reach for the handle, a surge of doubt rushes over me. I don't think I can do this anymore. I don't even know what I'll say when I get in there. I pull out my phone as I cross to the park opposite and find a bench. With shaky hands, I type a text.

> I don't know if I can do this.

Harriet's name flashes on my phone immediately with an incoming call.

"Where are you? If you need me, I'll be there in a

heartbeat," Harriet's reassuring voice sounds down the phone.

"I'm in London."

"Okay, maybe not a heartbeat, but say the word and I'll be on my way. I mean it."

"Thanks, babe, I just need a pep talk, and then I'll be on my way home again."

"Talk to me then, what's going on? Why don't you think you can do this?" Her soothing voice immediately calms me.

The past two weeks have been tough on both of us. Since Diane broke the news to me that I won't be getting a promotion at all, I've found it really hard to be positive about my career. I've done the bare minimum of my job, the part I get paid to do, and Di hasn't even noticed.

Harriet has though, and I know she is finding it tough just letting me get on with it. Even though I've been acting like a moody bastard on occasion, she's always there to comfort me or give me a reassuring hug whenever I've needed it, no questions asked.

Our relationship is the only thing keeping me sane right now. When we're together, it's the only thing that feels right. Until the guilt hits that I'm keeping this from her. I need to come clean about everything, and I intend to as soon as I get home, no matter the outcome.

"I'm outside his office."

"You don't have to do this, you know. From what you've told me, you don't owe him anything. But if it's something you need to do for yourself, I believe in you."

"I'm scared. I'm scared I'll tell him exactly how I feel and he won't care."

"If he doesn't care, then that's on him. You're an amazing person, and if he doesn't want to make the effort to find that out, then more fool him. He's the one missing out on you. He's the one that's missing how kind and loyal and loving you are. He's the one missing how strong and funny you are. You're the light in the darkness, Liam. You're my light, don't let him dim that."

"I love you."

"I love you too. Now, do what you need to do and come home to me. I think we both could do with a talk."

"I'll call you when I get on the train home," I promise, and we hang up.

With an injection of confidence, I stand and walk directly to the door, not wavering one bit. I grip the brass doorknob and push. It slowly creaks open, leading to a steep staircase.

As I climb to the first floor, I take in the various posters from Whitton Productions, many of which I've worked on in my time at the company. It's the first hint that this office is involved in the stage.

As I reach the top, I'm faced with a frosted-glass door with 'Whitton Productions' etched into it.

The receptionist doesn't look up when I enter, instead she continues typing on the computer as the phone rings and rings in the background.

She's young and looks like she really couldn't give a fuck.

I stand on the other side of her desk for a few seconds and clear my throat when she doesn't acknowledge that I'm standing in front of her.

"Do you have an appointment?" Her voice is monotone as she keeps her eyes locked on her screen.

"I'm Liam Wright, I'm here to see my dad."

"Do you have an appointment?" she repeats a little more sternly, as if I misunderstood her the first time.

"I'm his son, do I need an appointment?" I'm starting to get really annoyed at this girl.

She turns slowly to look at me for the first time, her face stoic as she takes me in.

"He's very busy today. I don't know if he has time to squeeze in another meeting." As she says the words, I hear a giggle coming from his office.

"Is he in there?" I point to the door behind her, and she nods ever so slightly. "Ask him if he'll see me."

"I can't—"

"Pick up the phone and ask if he'll see his son. Because I am not leaving here until I've spoken to him."

She lets out a sigh and picks up the phone on her desk. I hear him grumble 'oh, for fuck's sake' as his office phone rings.

"Mr Whitton, I've got a man here to see you. He says he's your son." She covers the receiver with her hand as she turns to me. "What's your name?"

"Liam Wright. As far as I'm aware I'm his only son." I'm quickly losing my patience.

"Liam Wright. Yes… okay… that's no problem. I'll check your calendar and let him know."

"Mr Whitton is in back-to-back meetings today, but I can schedule a meeting in October," she says confidently as though that's remotely acceptable.

"That's three months away."

At least she has the grace to look sorry for me this time.

My own dad is refusing to see me even though he knows I've travelled all this way. It's equal parts embarrassing, heart-breaking and infuriating. When I hear the woman laugh again from behind his office door, followed by his low rumbling, the familiarity hits me.

No fucking way!

I look between the receptionist and the door and weigh up my options.

Fuck it.

"Excuse me, you can't go in there," the receptionist says as I storm towards the door. I pay no attention to her.

I know I shouldn't make decisions like this based on emotions, but I don't care anymore, I'm done being seen but not heard. I'm done being a doormat. I'm done being played like a fool.

I swing open the door, slamming it back against the wall in the process.

Looking at Dad now, it's apparent how long it's been since I saw him last; if I didn't know this was his office, I might not even recognise him.

Di is sitting on his desk in front of him, her feet resting on the arms of his chair with her skirt around her stomach and her white blouse hanging open revealing her bra. Although they quickly cover themselves, they don't even have the decency to pretend to be embarrassed, instead they both glare at me.

"Liam!" Di scolds me as she holds her blouse closed, her face like thunder.

"What. The. Actual. Fuck!" I shout, losing all ability to keep cool.

"I could say the same to you, young man!" Dad booms as he stands and buttons his trousers back up. "Barging in on me like this when you were advised I was in meetings."

Meetings, fucking meetings?

My heart thunders in my ears, my hands are shaking, and I feel as though I'm about to explode.

I can't believe this, if I thought I was angry before, I'm livid now.

"Young man? I'm thirty years old, not a child. And you said you were in meetings not fucking an employee."

"Calm down, Liam," Di says calmly, having composed herself, but I can't even look at her, instead I glare into the cold, emotionally dead eyes of my father. "Let's have a cup of tea and talk about this."

"You can't make time to see your own son, but this you make time for?"

"We can explain," Di tries to reason with me, but it just sets me off on a rampage.

"Explain what? You've been telling me not to get involved with Harriet, a woman I've been in love with since the second I met her, because it'll jeopardise my career and you've been fucking my dad the whole time? Christ, you're such a hypocrite, Diane."

"How many times do we need to tell you we're protecting you? She's bad news. She got fired for having an affair with her director's husband because she thought she could use it to further her career. How do you think she got that part in the first place? She's calculating and conniving, Liam. What do you think she's going to do when she finds out who you are?"

"Whatever bullshit you've been fed about Harriet isn't true." Although I don't know the story, I know my girlfriend, and I know she'd never screw around for a better part.

"She's trying to take advantage of you, Liam. Why can't you see that? You're being manipulated and you're too blind to see it."

Dad interrupts as if I'm the idiot here. "Did she send you here?"

"She didn't send me here. She doesn't know who I am for fuck's sake, just like no one else knows that I exist! Your receptionist didn't even know you had a son." I point through the open door to where the receptionist sits, pretending she isn't listening to all this drama. "I'm sick of being kept as your dirty little secret and I am sick of being under your control."

"As long as you're working in the job I worked so hard to get you, you'll follow my rules, boy," Dad booms.

"Then I quit!" The relief of saying those words out loud to both Dad and Di engulfs me.

I'm finally free.

A burst of laughter spills out of me involuntarily.

I'm free and I can't wait to tell Harriet!

"You can't quit. You can't give up your career for some girl. You're a Whitton, you'll never get another job in this industry if you turn your back on your family. I'll make sure of it."

"Liam, think about it," Di pleads. "You're ruining your life over a girl."

I pause, holding the glass door open as I look back to a panic-stricken pair.

"I'm not giving it up for Harriet. I'm giving it up for me because I don't deserve any of the shit you put me through!" I stand taller. "I'm cutting all ties with you, Dad, because you don't deserve to have me in your life after everything you've done. And you, Diane, you don't deserve to have me as your lackey while you shag your way to the top. So, fuck you and fuck your job!"

CHAPTER THIRTY-SEVEN
Harriet

After tonight's show, a quick glance at the message on my phone tells me he got off the train at Durham and will be home in half an hour, so I hurry through the process of removing my mic, wig and costume to make my way over to him.

I carefully hand my wig to the wig assistants Sharon and Carmen and pass Rachael on my way out of the room. She smirks at me with a sinister glint in her eyes before swinging the door closed. It's an old building so it doesn't quite fit in the doorframe anymore, leaving a gap.

"Oh my god, girls guess what," she says, her voice clear as day through the small crack she left. "Harriet and Liam are shagging."

I'm rooted to the spot, my blood running cold.

"No way!" Sharon and Carmen gasp.

"You know why she left her last company, right?" Rachael laughs. "I know a guy in London, he worked with her. And he told me it was because she was caught shagging the director's husband. Apparently, he was her drama teacher and she seduced him." Cue more gasps from the gossiping trio. I should barge in there and tell them they've it all wrong, but I can't move as the walls start to cave in around me. "That's not even the worst part. She told him she'd tell his wife if he didn't get her that lead role in the West End. She clearly thinks she can shag her way to the top wherever she is. No wonder she's set her sights on Liam, she obviously doesn't know Liam has no pull with the Whittons."

"I bet she planned it from the moment she realised who his dad is," Carmen says. "Poor guy is so naive he doesn't even realise she's using him."

The panic builds as I try to make sense of this, but I can't make it add up.

"I don't know, they seem to really like each other," Sharon steps in in my defence.

"Oh please, she's happy because she's dating a Whitton," Rachael says bitterly. "Liam has gone to London for a meeting with his dad and Diane today. I wouldn't be surprised if she went from swing to principal lead overnight. The man has no backbone. If she asks him, she'll get it... Oh, Sharon, don't look at me like that. This is my job on the line. If she takes my role, what will I do?"

My heart is thundering in my ears and the walls warp around me.

Liam is a Whitton?

His family own this production company?

His family own this theatre?

That can't be right. I would know this. I'm his girlfriend, he would have told me.

I text Jayne and ask her to pick me up asap and I'll explain everything in the car. Then I stumble back to my dressing room on autopilot. My brain is elsewhere, lost in a montage of everything he's ever said to me, and the more I think about our conversations surrounding his dad, the more obvious it becomes.

He knows everything about this place, about this company. He said his dad got him the job here and of course he did. It's his dad's company.

Dread prickles the back of my neck, as the severity of this sinks in. Before long, the gossip will spread and I'll be laughed out of here.

I can't believe I let this happen again.

"Are you okay?" Katie asks when I swing open our door, my eyes brimming with tears as I teeter on the edge of a complete breakdown. "What's wrong?"

"I don't feel very well, I'm going to go home." I quickly pack up all my belongings from my dressing table before turning to my locker and clearing it out quickly.

"This doesn't look like you're going home for the day, Harriet. Talk to me."

I can feel Katie watching me with concern as I move with shaky hands. I can't even look at her. Obviously, she knows, she's his cousin. I thought she was my friend, but of course her loyalties lie with her family.

"Why won't you look at me? What happened?"

I turn to her, and worry etches deeper into her forehead when she processes my impending breakdown.

"I need you to give Liam a message for me," I say, tears

streaming down my face as the shock wears off and the pain sinks in.

"Anything."

"Tell him I know all about his dad." I don't wait for her response as I walk out of the room, tossing my bag over my shoulder.

"Harriett, wait!" She runs down the corridor to catch up with me. "You need to talk to him about this, let him explain."

"He's had plenty of time to explain, Katie, and so have you. Am I the only one that didn't know?" I shout as more tears fall. I swipe them away, angry at myself for getting into this position and angry at her for allowing it too. "Does Zach know? Has everyone been laughing at me behind my back this entire time?"

"He never wanted to hurt you, just give him a chance to tell the whole story. It's not a big deal."

"It's a huge deal, Katie. You should have told me!"

Tears well up in her eyes as we face each other in the corridor. Zach skids around the corner, out of breath and half dressed in his trousers and socks before jogging to Katie's side. "You both should have told me."

"It's not our story to tell, Harriet," Zach says as Katie and I cry. He doesn't need to ask me what's wrong; he already knows.

"I'm so sorry, Harriet," Katie says, her own pain evident. "Please don't go. Don't leave because of this."

Deep down, I understand why she didn't tell me, I really do, but I can't think about that right now. All I need is to get away from this place and put as much distance between me and this whole fucked-up situation as possible.

So, I walk away. And I don't look back.

CHAPTER THIRTY-EIGHT
Liam

As I pay for my parking, my phone rings in my pocket. Juggling everything, I see it's Katie ringing and ignore it. By the time I get to my car a few minutes later, I have four missed calls from Katie and Zach and another comes through as soon as my phone connects to the Bluetooth in my car.

"Hey, sorry, I was connecting my phone. I know I haven't called to update you yet, but I wanted to speak to Harriet fir—"

"Liam, something's wrong," Katie says with a sniffle.

"What's wrong?" Panic surges through my body.

"It's Harriet…she…she already knows." My blood turns to ice in my veins as Katie lets out a sob. "I told you this would happen, Liam. I told you it would come back on all of us. On me and Zach! You should have told her weeks ago!"

There's a rustling noise on the other end of the phone, but I barely notice as I sit in my car, still parked up at Durham station.

"Alright, mate." Zach's voice comes on the line sounding much calmer than Katie's.

"What's happened?"

"She overheard Rachael talking to Sharon and Carmen… Look, it's a long story and I don't think any of us know the truth, but I know Harriet, and I know she would never do what they're saying she did."

"They were talking about the director's husband, weren't they?" The numbness begins to take over as realisation sets in.

"Yeah."

"When she left, they made her sign an NDA. Innocent people don't make people sign NDAs like they did to Harriet. There's more to it, there has to be."

"I don't doubt that. But, Liam, the rumours are out now. And so is the fact that you and Harriet are together."

My head drops. "Fuck."

"That's not all…" he says. "Everyone knows who your dad is because Rachael told them…"

"…And they think she's doing it again," I finish. "Fuck!" I bang my hands against the steering wheel. "Where is she?"

"She packed her stuff and left. She was really upset, mate. We tried to talk to her but… Like Katie said, we kept your secret and she sort of… well… she has a right to be angry at us."

"Where is she?" I ask again.

"She's at home," Zach says.

I disconnect the call quickly, without so much as a goodbye, and drive towards Harriet's house, dialling her number through the car.

The call goes to voicemail, so I try Jayne next.

"I warned you. I told you not to hurt her," Jayne snaps the second she answers, venom in her voice like I've never heard before. "You *promised* you wouldn't hurt her. You kept this from her, knowing fine well how this would look for her if it got out. You made Katie keep your secret! And Zach. Everyone she trusted."

"Jayne, I can explain. I need to talk to her, please I'm begging you," I plead.

"I'm sure you can explain, but why do you deserve to? You've been lying to her for months!"

"I love her, Jayne. Please give me a chance to prove that to her." My voice cracks at the words, panic filling my chest. "I can't lose her."

She pauses, considering my words. "How did Rachael find out about London?"

"I-I don't know. I don't even know what happened in London."

"Well, everyone else thinks they know and it's all because of that bitch spreading rumours."

"Zach told me what they're saying about us, about her. But I know none of it's true."

She pauses. I assume she's conferring silently with Harriet because a moment later Jayne sighs.

"Harriet had a teacher at college and after she graduated, they stayed in touch. A few years later he began to feed her all this bullshit about her being the one and saying that he loved her despite their age gap. They dated in secret for a few years because he told her the industry wouldn't take him seriously if people knew he fell in love with a student, and she believed it. She cared about him and didn't want to see his career ruined," Jayne says and I think I can piece together where this is going.

"He got her this amazing role in the West End. Her big break. He came to the show one night and surprised her in her dressing room. She didn't know he was married and living a double life until his wife, the director of the show she was starring in, found them together."

"Shit." I sigh, not knowing what else to say to this bombshell.

"The snake told everyone that Harriet had seduced him that night, that he was a weak man who made a mistake. He had the nerve to put it on his wife. She worked long hours and didn't pay him enough attention, and she believed it!

"This man was Harriet's drama teacher. She trusted him, and he groomed her for years, kept her as his plaything, and as soon as he was caught, threw her to the wolves to protect himself. People believed him. She was the one they talked about, the one they blamed and called a slut. She was the one who lost her job, her dream and her spark."

"I had no idea," I say, pulling to the side of the road. I sit with my head in my hands as my brain is bombarded with questions.

If I had known about this, would I have told her about Dad earlier? I honestly don't know.

I didn't keep my identity from her to hurt her or because I thought she would try to use me; I know she never would. I kept it from her because I'm ashamed that I let him take advantage of his position over me for all these years. I was embarrassed that I lay down and took his abuse with no questions asked, all because I was scared to confront the truth that he never wanted anything to do with me in the first place other than to have me as a possession.

"The guy paid her off to go quietly, to not tell his wife the truth about the extent of their relationship. She just wanted to get the out of there as soon as possible, so she took the money, signed an NDA and came home. She legally couldn't tell you. Do you know what the worst part of all this is? Even though she's the victim here, she still genuinely believes it was her fault."

"Jayne. I…" I have no idea what to say. "I can't lose her, I love her." My voice is barely above a whisper as my emotions wrap me in a choke hold.

I hear a door close on the other side of the phone.

"Listen," she says, her voice softer. "When I picked her up on that first day at the theatre, I saw a glimpse of the part of my sister I thought was lost. Even more so since you got together. You helped bring her back out of herself again. You showed her that not every man is a spineless prick. And I believe you when you say you love her, and you didn't mean to hurt her. But let me offer you some free advice. Let her have tonight to wallow, then tomorrow, when she's calmed down, I'll try get her to speak to you so you can explain."

"Thank you." I swallow the ball of emotion lodged in my throat. "I appreciate it."

CHAPTER THIRTY-NINE
Harriet

When I wake up the next morning, I momentarily forget the events of last night. I half expect to see Liam curled up around me. And then it all comes rushing back when I see that my sister is stretched diagonally across my bed as I cling on to the edge for dear life.

Next comes the pain.

I've read about heartbreak; I've seen it in movies and acted it out on stage. But until this moment, I realise I've never felt it before.

Everything about me aches. I'm mentally and physically drained.

After everything kicked off, word spread around the company quickly and soon my phone was lit up with notifications, people texting and calling me. Some of them were nice and caring, asking if I'm okay. Most of them not so much.

Social media is blowing up too. People I considered to be friends are publicly calling me a whore or a gold digger and take it upon themselves to tell their version of my story. They claim that one time, they could excuse as a mistake, but twice… well, now it's a pattern.

I drag myself out of bed and pad to the bathroom to shower,

hoping it will wash away the tension I'm carrying. I go through the daily motions as if I'm not falling apart inside; I brush my teeth, put on some make-up and blow dry my hair. I sit downstairs, ignoring the looks that pass between Mam and Jayne as we enjoy a coffee.

"Harriet," Mam starts. "Do you want to talk about it?"

"Not really."

"Liam called me again this morning," Jayne says. "He's going to stop by later. He wants to talk and I really think you should hear him out."

I stare at my sister in disbelief. "You spoke to him? Why?"

"Because you've shut out the world. He's hurting just as bad as you are right now, and to be honest, he's fucking terrified—"

"Jayne, language," Mam interjects.

"He's scared of this abuse you're getting online; he's scared in case someone hurts you and rightly so, because we are too," she says, looking at Mam, who scooches closer to me and squeezes my hand.

"I can handle it. It's been twelve hours. Give me a break."

"He told me he never wanted to hurt you, and I believe him." As she says that, the doorbell rings and I glare at my sister.

Mam leaves the room to answer it before leading a rough looking Liam into the kitchen.

"Jayne and I are going to visit Dad. I'll take you down for the afternoon slot, okay?" Mam says, kissing me on the cheek as they leave us alone.

"Can we talk?" Liam asks.

"I don't think I have a choice, do I?" I say coldly, doing my best to suppress the heartache.

"Harriet, I'm so sorry. We can fix this together. All of it."

"There's nothing left to fix, Liam, I'm ruined! I told you! I told you weeks ago that my career wouldn't survive if this happened again," I say, the tears pushing at the walls that contain them. "And now look... I've been branded a whore and no one knows the true story. With him, the story is that I'm the gold digger going after a married man, and with you, I'm using you to get to your dad. But the reality is, I'm the victim here." My voice finally breaks as the tears overflow, streaking in heavy streams down my face. "I'm the one who was left shattered by him, jobless and friendless with zero self-confidence.

"But you know what, I'd go through that a thousand times over if it meant never having to feel like I do now. You broke my trust and you broke my heart. And I don't even think I'm mad at you because in the light of day, I can see why you kept it a secret. It's me I'm mad at because I let myself fall in love with you when I should have known better."

"Harriet..." He takes a step towards me, flinching as I recoil away from him.

"I think you should go."

"I won't give up on us. I can't just walk away and pretend that we didn't fall in love, Harriet. I can't walk away from our relationship when it's the best thing to happen to me." His own voice is hoarse with emotion.

I wipe the tears from my cheeks and pull the walls back up

around me, just enough so I can end the conversation.

"Then it's a good job I can, because I'm done."

"I can sack them all," Robert says when he calls me later that afternoon. It's nice to have him on my side; he always seemed indifferent to the cast, but in the past five minutes he's morphed into sort of a big brother figure. "I mean it, I'm about two minutes away from sacking everyone. If I could sack Liam too, I would."

"No, you wouldn't, this show is important to you and it's sold out for another six weeks of shows, and you wouldn't disappoint the audiences like that."

He mumbles in agreement. I wouldn't want him to jeopardise the show like that, or the cast and crew that have stood up for me publicly.

"I hate my moral compass sometimes," he says dramatically, making me laugh. "I want you to know that they are being disciplined for what's happened though."

"I wish that made me feel better, Robert." I sigh. "Did anyone say where the information came from? About what happened in London? The only person that should have known was Mr Whitton."

"Harriet, I don't think you want to know."

"It was him, wasn't it?" I ask, although it's a rhetorical question, I know it was him.

"Kind of," Robert confirms, regret in his tone. "He and Liam got into a big fight down in London and you were brought up. The receptionist heard everything and before we knew it, the gossip had made it back to Rachael. For what it's worth, they know the truth now. He didn't go into specifics, but Liam laid into them all about an hour ago."

"What about the rest of the internet? They all think I'm a home-wrecking, gold-digging, whore."

"This will pass, Harriet. But in the meantime, take some time off and look after yourself and come back when you're ready."

"Thanks, Robert, I will," I say as we hang up, although I know in my heart, I'll never be able to step into that theatre again.

CHAPTER FORTY
Harriet

"I hate seeing you like this," Dad says as I sit at his bedside in the hospice. It's been a week since my life fell apart again and I've sat by his side every day doing my best to hide my pain.

I'm not doing a great job of it, but it's a good distraction, masking one heartbreak with another.

Today is one of Dad's good days, where his pain is manageable and he's conscious enough between naps to have a conversation. Much of the week he's slept or been in too much pain to acknowledge that I'm even here.

That's one thing they don't tell you about terminal illness –that one day a person can be alert and smiling and happy and the next be so close to death you say goodbye before you leave the room even for just a second. Today feels like somewhere in between.

"I'm sorry, I didn't know you were awake again." I sit up, leaning across to take his hand.

"Do you want to talk about it?" His forehead wrinkles in a pained frown and his voice is weak as though it's taking all his energy to form a sentence.

"I'm great, Dad." It's a pointless lie; I'm a daddy's girl, he can read me like a book.

"Liam came to visit me this morning." I try my best not to react but even the sound of his name sends a knife plunging into my heart.

"Oh, lovely," I say in my best attempt at being normal. I haven't told Dad about the breakup; I don't want him to die worried about me.

"He came to apologise to me. A few weeks ago, he promised me he'd spend his life making you happy, but instead, he inadvertently broke your heart."

"He said that?" I'm taken aback by this new information.

"He also said that you're refusing to speak to him. He's a mess, sweetheart." If at all possible, knowing Liam is a mess after our breakup makes me feel worse still.

"Did he tell you what he did?"

"He told me everything."

I look down at my hand while I try to compose my thoughts.

"I let it happen again, Dad." My voice is quiet and unsteady, and I feel like I'm five years old, telling him about the kid who picked on me that day at school. Dad always said the right things; he always made things better. There are so many things I wish I could tell my younger self, and one of them is not to take those moments of comfort from my dad for granted. "I thought Liam was different, but I was wrong. We both have flaws, but I can't ignore the fact he hid that part of his life from me."

"I don't love that he kept something from you, but seeing

your reaction this week, does it really surprise you that he didn't tell you? My girl, I love you, but you can't half overreact. He was afraid to tell you until he knew how to. From what he told me, his dad has been emotionally abusing him since he was a kid. He has wounds he needs to work on much like you do. And, like you, he's good at hiding those wounds."

"Its London all over again, Dad, although this time I don't think my reputation or my career will survive."

"Of course, it will. This is nothing like London, so instead of looking at the similarities why not look at the differences. That man in London would never have come to your parents' house to move heaven and earth to have me at that show. If Liam used his influence or connections to the theatre to get me there so I could watch you perform one last time, then I don't begrudge him that at all."

I nod and swipe away the rogue tears that have slipped from my eyes and down my cheeks.

"I knew the first time I met him, when he sat across from me in our living room telling me that plan, that he cared for you even then. I saw the way he looked at you that night too, how seeing you so happy made him happy. Stop sabotaging yourself because you think it's the right thing to do, because it's not. You can't throw away a relationship because of one mistake, otherwise, you and your sister wouldn't exist at all."

I laugh, because even now when he's so sick, he's doing all he can to cheer me up. That's just the kind, loving man my dad is.

"Thanks, Dad." He squeezes my hand weakly. "What will

I do when you're not here anymore?"

I'm openly crying now; tears tumble down my cheeks in a steady flow as I sniff and wipe my nose on my jumper.

Dad weakly hands me a tissue from his table, knocking my sleeves away from my nose like I'm a toddler. "My girl, I'll always be here watching over you from wherever I go next."

"I love you, Dad," I look up to see Mam standing in the doorway, wiping her own tears from her eyes as she watches our exchange.

"I love you too, Harriet," Dad says, his grip is strong as his hand lingers meaningfully in mine. "Go and take a break and get yourself a coffee. It looks like you haven't slept for days." I laugh through my sniffles. "You're still beautiful though."

As I'm standing at the coffee machine, watching the cheap instant coffee pour into a tiny polystyrene cup, a buzzing alarm grabs my attention.

I know that alarm. I've heard it a few times since I've been here this week. It's not overly loud, sounding more like a mobile ringing on vibrate as a dashboard flashes at the nurse's station.

I don't know how, but this time I know that the alarm is for me.

I look out into the hallway and see Jayne standing frozen at the opposite end of the corridor. Both of us look at the tiny red light flashing above Dad's door and our faces mirror each other's panic.

"Dad!" I shout as I run to his door, not knowing what I'll do when I get there. There's nothing I can do; I know what that alarm means and I'm powerless.

Jayne and I arrive at the same time. My eyes land on Dad's sleeping frame, my mam's face buried into the side of the love of her life as she weeps.

Grief pours out of me like an avalanche, building and building as the realisation sets in, burying me in a darkness that I'm not ready for.

CHAPTER FORTY-ONE
Harriet

My phone buzzes on my bedside table, but I don't even look at it just like the many other phone calls I've had. In the nine days since dad died, I haven't spoken to anyone other than sending a text to Robert to tell him I needed more time off.

I should let them know I have no intention of returning at all, but quite honestly, I couldn't give two fucks – it all seems so small and petty on the scale of things.

Katie has been staying over most nights with Jayne and I'm glad she's got someone to look after her. As much as I want to offer my little sister that support, I know that mentally, I'm in no fit state. I'm drowning in my own grief, and I miss my dad. I want him back more than anything, and the pain of knowing I'll never see him again overshadows everything else in my life.

I told myself I'd let myself feel this way until the funeral and then I'd try to heal, but today is the funeral and I don't think I'm ready yet. I don't think I'm ready to let go of this empty feeling of sorrow and I can't see a time where I will be.

The doorbell rings as I scrutinise my reflection in the full-length mirror. I've lost weight; my dress doesn't fit as nicely as it used to, and I can see that the muscles I developed from dancing all my life have started to wither away.

I sigh when the doorbell rings again and Mam shouts for me to answer it. I scoop up my black strappy shoes, letting them dangle from my fingers as I take them with me.

Truthfully, the last person I expect to see standing on my front step when I open the door is Liam, but here he is, dressed in a black suit with his beard combed neatly and his hair in place.

Emotion overwhelms me the moment he turns, and our eyes meet for the first time since I walked away from him in my kitchen.

He catches me before I crumble to the ground, holding me with his strong and steady arms as I weep uncontrollably into his chest. I haven't allowed myself to think about him more than a handful of times.

My dreams however are a different story. Whenever his face pops up in my dreams, it's either a painful reminder of how it ended between us, or I wake up having forgotten that we broke up in the first place.

That's the worst part, when the early morning fog clears from my brain, and I remember that he isn't mine anymore.

"Harriet." He rubs comforting circles on my back when he manages to get me into the sitting room and onto the sofa.

"What are you doing here?" I choke out, swiping the tears from my eyes and leaning back so I can look at him properly. He looks tired but still as gorgeous as ever. "I know that things didn't work out with us, and that was my fault, but I still care about you. I'm still here for you, at the very least as your friend."

The word friend echoes in my brain and I remember a time when he told me being my friend wasn't enough for him.

After the service at the crematorium and our gathering in the garden of remembrance, we all head down the road to Dad's local pub. The function room is packed with familiar and not so familiar faces all here to celebrate my dad. I'm filled with a sense of pride that he was loved and admired by so many.

It's an exhausting day as I smile and laugh at fond memories people have of him. Other stories of his kindness and generosity make me want to cry, but I manage to hold it all back.

By the time eight p.m. comes around, there is no sign of the celebration of his life stopping and people are starting to get a little tipsy, including Jayne who has already polished off one bottle of wine to herself as Katie supports her.

Me, on the other hand, I've been nursing the same glass of rosé since I got here. I just don't feel like drinking, but at the same time I feel like I need something to hold.

"Why don't you go home, sweetheart?" Mam suggests when Liam excuses himself to go to the bathroom. He's been by my side all day, holding me together when all I want to do is fall part, even though neither of us have really exchanged any real words, both of us choosing to ignore our situation so I can get through the afternoon. "You've been here all day. Jayne is fine with Katie and your aunties and uncles will be here for hours yet, so I'm happy to stay."

"Are you sure you don't mind, Mam?"

"Of course not. You always were the sensitive one, your dad knew that, and he'd hate to see you staying here for the sake of everyone else. Get yourself home," she says as Liam arrives back at the table.

"Can you drive me?" I ask him softly.

"Come on, let's go home, babe," he says, probably out of habit more than anything else, but oh how I wish he meant that.

"Will you stay with me tonight?" I ask as we emerge into the cool, late summer air.

"Anything you need."

CHAPTER FORTY TWO
Liam

Harriet pulls off her shoes and groans as her bare feet stretch on the hard wood floor.

In complete silence, we go through the motions of getting a couple of glasses of water from the kitchen and climbing the stairs to her bedroom. We undress together and brush our teeth side by side at her sink like we have many times before. If the giant cloud wasn't hanging above us, it would probably feel normal.

When we're alone in her bedroom, I close the distance between us, wrapping my arms around her as I breathe her in, inhaling as much of her as possible.

"Liam," she whispers as her blue-green eyes connect with mine.

There's so much I want to say, but the words don't come. Instead, I follow her lead when she tugs me towards her, pressing her mouth to mine in a slow, earth-shattering kiss. Our lips move together in a familiar pattern as though no time has passed.

I open up to her, allowing her tongue to sweep over mine as I drink her in. I've missed this so much, this feeling of belonging that I only have with her. Desire spreads over my body and although I know in the back of my mind that this is a bad idea, I give in to the temptation of deepening our kiss.

Since I can't make the words I need to say to her come out, I pour everything into this kiss in a silent conversation only we can understand.

I love her. I miss her. And I'm sorry I broke us.

She presses herself against me, walking me backwards until my legs hit her bed and I fall to a seated position, shifting back slightly. I give her more room to climb on top of me so she's straddling my lap, holding her as close to my body as possible.

Our hands are all over each other, mine are in her hair and on her back before sliding over her bum, pulling her down on to the part of my body that throbs with need. Her head tips back in pleasure as she feels me hard beneath her.

She's wearing my t-shirt. The one she stole the night we got together, and she looks just as amazing in it tonight.

Although it's been three weeks since we were last together, it feels like just yesterday that I had her in my arms like this. She grinds against me again, and I gasp at the sensation, needing to be inside her.

I stand with her in my arms, the flip her onto her back with her head on her pillow, returning my mouth to hers. She arches into me as we grind into one another, but when my name falls from her lips in a breathy moan, I wake from the haze as though a bucket of ice-cold water has been dropped on my head.

I can't believe I'm about to do this when I've finally got the woman I love in my arms again.

"What are we doing Harriet?" I pull away from her ever so

slightly – it's the hardest thing I've ever had to do, but it's necessary. Our breathing is ragged, and I don't want to let go of her, but neither of us are thinking straight and I don't want to do something she might end up regretting.

"This is the first time I've felt something other than pain for weeks, I need it." She pulls me by my neck to kiss her again, although this time it's all her.

I need it.

It, not me.

"I can't have sex with you when you're using it as a distraction," I whisper when her eyes meet mine. I can't do it. No matter how much I want to be with her, it wouldn't be right.

"You're rejecting me?" Her unsteady voice is laced with pain. Pushing me aside, she scrambles from her bed and paces the floor of her room. I can tell she's embarrassed, but she needn't be. "I'm literally handing myself over to you for a night of no-strings-attached sex and you're rejecting me?"

"I'm not taking advantage of your vulnerability." I drag my hand through my hair as I try to put this delicately. "And I don't want no-strings sex with you. I want all the strings, Harriet, every last one of them."

"You don't want me because I'm vulnerable?" Her voice is raised, and tears glaze her eyes.

"That's what you're taking from what I said!?" I'm so annoyed that that's the part she is focusing on that I take a calming breath and go for the truth. "Harriet, I miss you more than anything. Of course, I want you, I love you! There isn't a day that goes by where I don't wish that I could go back in time and do things differently. I wish I could take away your pain. I wish I could distract you, believe me. But take it from someone who has been where you are, that's not how grief works, you can't hide from it. I'll do my best to comfort you respectfully while you feel this way, because the way you're feeling right now is normal and justified, I promise you."

She looks at me stunned, so I take advantage of her silence and continue.

"I've been speaking to Jayne over the past two weeks, a lot actually because she's really worried about you. I know you're not eating or sleeping, and I know you have no intention of going back to the show even though we both know you're happiest on stage." The tears are now rolling down her cheeks, so I grab a tissue from a box on her bedside table and go to her. "I'll support you no matter what you decide. I'll be right there by your side for as long as you need me, but until you start being true to yourself, I think it's best we stay friends."

She's silent for a while as she processes my words.

"You're right. I don't know how to live without him." Her voice is quiet when she sits on the edge of her bed. Her hands twist in her lap, so I kneel in front of her, looking up into her eyes and offering her my hands. She takes them and entwines her fingers through mine as her tears flow freely.

I move next to her on the bed, pulling her to me and holding her as she cries, doing my best not to fall apart myself.

"I know, Harriet," I say, holding her tightly. "I know."

I help her into bed and climb in next to her, then turn off her bedside lamp, plunging us into darkness.

"For tonight, can we pretend we're okay?" she asks as she snuggles up close to my side, her soft palm lingering on my cheek.

"Yeah." I tilt her chin with my fingers and brush my lips lightly against hers. This time, our kiss is tender and slow, and neither of us deepen it or let our hands wander because this closeness and comfort is exactly what we need, even though we both know it can't last.

CHAPTER FORTY-THREE
Liam

Waking up next to Harriet is torture. My body clearly hasn't gotten the memo that we aren't together, because the moment she sits up and looks down at me with her tired eyes that scream morning sex, it's crying for me to pull her down on top of me and have my way with her.

I know she has the same thoughts because her neck flushes pink and her breath hitches when I let my eyes trail down her body.

"You'll be going on tour in a few weeks. Are you excited?" She makes small talk across the breakfast bar as we sip on our morning coffee. I'm confused until I see she genuinely doesn't know that I quit.

"Jayne hasn't told you?"

"Told me what?"

"When I confronted my dad in London, I quit. I told him to go fuck himself and to fuck his job too."

"You did?" Her eyes are as wide as saucers.

"I couldn't work for him anymore. I'd had enough long before then I just never did anything about it… The day we met was the closest I'd come to quitting for real. I found out I didn't have the promotion I was promised year after year, and I was fed up. I was on my way to tell Di when I bumped into you in the street. I felt what we had immediately, so I stayed because something deep down told me you were worth it. And I know things haven't worked out for us, but I'd do it all again for that brief time we had together."

"You stayed for me even though you hated it?" she asks, her eyes softening.

"I told myself I was staying for you, that's how I justified it. I could have just asked for your number that morning or had Katie set us up, but telling myself I was staying for you gave me an excuse not to look at the real reason I couldn't leave." I take a deep breath. "I wasn't aware of the emotional abuse he and Diane put me through until I started talking to someone about it recently."

Therapy was a big step for me and although I have a long way to go, I finally feel like I can breathe enough to talk about my life.

"I didn't tell him I was travelling to see him that day because I knew he'd tell me he was too busy. After I'd spoken to you, I gathered the courage to go to his office. He was right there, I could hear him behind the door, and yet, he told his receptionist he wouldn't meet with me. He was on the other side of the door and he still turned me away. I lost my temper and barged in to find him and Diane going at it on his desk. I told them both to fuck the job and that I quit."

"What the hell!" Her eyes widen once more. "They were together?"

"Apparently so." I nod. "I didn't ask them the mechanics of their relationship, but I did call Di a hypocrite when she tried to turn the whole thing back against you. I'm sorry, Harriet. I should have been honest from the beginning, but ever since I was a kid I've been hidden away like some shameful secret. Since I was seven years old, they told me that the world can't know who my dad is because people will try to use me, they'll try to extort me and other bullshit. They fucked me up so much I actually believed them. Until I met you."

"I'm so sorry, Liam, you didn't deserve that. I'm glad you're working through it." She pauses thoughtfully.

"Talk to me."

"What are you going to do now?" she asks.

"I've had some job offers. Turns out I'm not as bad at my job as my dad had me believe all these years. Some could take me on tour, a couple require relocating, so I have options. I'm selling Mam's house. I need a clean start somewhere that doesn't remind me of her and the bad shit we went through."

She nods, contemplating.

We sit in silence for a little while as we finish our coffee until the time comes for me to leave.

"Thank you for coming yesterday. I really needed that support." She awkwardly folds her arms and then unfolds them again.

"Anytime. You know where to find me if you need me, Harriet."

"Thank you, but I think you're right. I need a clean start too," she says as we reach her front step, her eyes glistening with tears.

She takes my face in her hands, stands on her tiptoes and kisses me softly. As we say our final goodbye, I can feel her warm tears running down her cheeks and I have to fight to keep from shedding my own. Because, as much as I don't want to, I know I'm the only one who can give her that clean start by walking away.

CHAPTER FORTY-FOUR
Harriet

Familiar voices drift in from the hallway as I lounge on the sofa where I've been for the past month, maybe two?

I prop myself up and glare at Katie who is wearing an extremely sheepish expression.

"Robert and Zach? Seriously?" I exclaim as she looks anywhere but my direction.

They file into the room led by Jayne and look around until their sympathetic eyes meet mine.

"Harriet, you look…" Robert says.

"As beautiful as ever," Zach finishes, narrowing his eyes at Robert in warning.

"I was going to say tragic," he continues with brutal honestly. He's not wrong, I suppose. I've worn the same t-shirt for three days now, my hair is a mess and I'm pretty sure the tomato sauce on my pyjama bottoms is from yesterday's breakfast. I swipe my hair away from my face and tuck it into the bobble that's holding my hair back in a messy… well, I can't even call it a bun, a bird's nest would be more representative of my appearance.

Although I've spoken to both Robert and Zach a few times since I quit the show, I've not yet seen them in person so I can't imagine what they think of me now.

After the show closed in Sunderland, they went on tour for six weeks. That was a few days after Dad's funeral and Katie's been back a week now, which is a relief since Jayne doesn't bother me as much about moving on when Katie is here.

"Right, here's the plan," Robert says, clapping his hands and taking charge like it's second nature. I suppose it is for him, it's what makes him a great director. "Shelley," he points to Mam, "you get her showered. Jayne, find her something to wear and sort her hair out. Katie, you're on music. Zach, you're in charge of booze."

"What on earth is going on?" I say as everyone springs into action.

"It's an intervention, sweetheart, your family and friends can't watch you self-destruct like this any longer." Mam nudges me out of the living room and up the stairs to the bathroom.

Opening my cabinet, she hands me a razor and a new shower scrunchie.

"Thanks," I say, looking down at them as if she's handed me a million pounds.

"Just shout if you need me," she says before leaving the room and leaving me to stare at my own reflection. It's not often I stare at myself in the mirror, which is why I'm so shocked to see how pale I am. My face has a grey tinge to it, and I know it's because I've stopped looking after myself, choosing to eat junk instead of a balanced meal, neglecting my hair and skin so much that the shine and glow have vanished.

My body is different too. I've never been typically thin,

ever since I hit puberty I've had curves, but there's no definition anymore. The muscles that had started to wilt at Dad's funeral are non-existent and my body doesn't feel like my own anymore. I don't feel as strong.

No wonder everyone is so worried about me because I don't resemble myself at all, inside or out.

Sighing, I step into the shower, letting the steaming hot water reinvigorate me. I shave the areas I've let go, scrub my skin almost raw with my salt scrub and opt for a second conditioning treatment on my dry, frizzy hair.

When I'm done, I find the clothes Jayne has picked out for me in my bedroom.

It's just a simple t-shirt and skinny jeans but as soon as I pull the clothes on, I feel more like myself again. Not quite one hundred per cent but it helps.

"Well now, don't you look beautiful," Robert says as Zach hands me some sort of cocktail.

The first sip has me wincing – I should have guessed it would be strong since Zach was in charge of the drinks – it's more vodka than anything else.

I ignore the fact it's not long after lunchtime on a Tuesday and take another generous swig, hoping it numbs the guilt bubbling up in my stomach.

"So... tell me about the tour," I say as we gather around the breakfast bar on tall stools. It dawns on me that the entire time they were away I didn't ask that once; I've been far too consumed by my own misery to think of them.

They exchange a loaded look between them.

"The tour was shit. Let's be frank," Zach says. Katie and Robert nod their agreement.

"Come on, it can't have been that bad," I say. "There have to have been some fun times."

"Without you and Liam, it didn't run as smooth." Katie shrugs. "Not to mention, the divide and tension between the company made it really awkward."

"I'm so sorry," I say. Everyone was looking forward to touring, and they didn't get that happy, exciting experience because I caused that rift.

"It wasn't you, Harriet," Robert says softly. "Word got around about how Liam's dad and Di have been treating him and since everyone loves Liam, they turned on Di. Besides, no one trusts Rachael anymore since she started the rumour about you, and that's definitely not your fault."

"Okay, I brought my karaoke machine, shall we have a go at musical theatre karaoke to lighten the mood?" Katie says, changing the subject and pulling me from the stool towards the living room before I start crying again.

"I don't think I have a choice, do I?" I laugh.

"Nope," she says, popping the last syllable. "Zach, bring the cocktail jugs while you're at it. It's going to be a messy afternoon."

It doesn't take too long for the alcohol to hit, and a few hours later, we're all pretty tipsy and fighting over the microphone.

"Katie, you've sung 'Popular' four times now, pick something else!" Jayne whines at her girlfriend and we all laugh.

"It's my fave and I'm finishing it!" Katie snaps back before picking back up without missing a beat.

When the song finishes, the playlist continues while we decide what song to tackle next.

"What about Robert and I sing 'Bad Idea' from Waitress?" I suggest, but I don't hear anyone's response.

The walls close in around me as I turn slowly towards the TV displaying the song I know immediately by the opening note. All eyes are on me as I watch the words appear on the screen for "As Long As You're Mine" from *Wicked*.

The gut-wrenching heartache bursts from nowhere and slams into me as I'm hurtled back in time to when Liam and I had our first date, the hour-long road trip to Hamsterley Forest when he sang with me for the first time and we talked about ridiculous things. I knew right then that I loved him and I'd give anything to go back and relive that day. Even if the end result was the same, without a doubt, I do all of it again.

A sob escapes me before I even realise I'm crying.

"I'm so sorry," I say over and over again as my friends rally around me.

"Hey, it's okay," Zach says, kneeling in front of me, his hands on my knees, as Jayne and Katie sit either side of me, taking a hand each. "It doesn't have to be like this, you know."

"It's for the best. He needed a clean break and so did I," I explain, although as every day passes, I doubt my decision more and more.

"I don't believe that for a second and I know you don't either," Zach says, looking me in the eye. "I saw him yesterday…" I want to shake Zach. I want to beg him to tell me Liam's okay. That this pain is worth it because he's not hurting anymore, but before I get that chance, he continues, "Harriet, he's miserable too, but he thinks this is what you want so he's trying to respect your wishes."

"He is?"

Zach nods.

"I still love him." My voice is barely above a whisper as Jayne and Katie sit either side of me, hugging me tightly.

"Then do something about it instead of wallowing here," Robert says sternly, giving me tough love and cutting off my waterworks. "Let's cut all the self-sacrificial nonsense, do you want him back?"

"Yeah." I wipe away the tears from my cheeks. "Yeah, I do."

"Okay, let's get him back then," Robert says simply. "We all need jobs, so… let's write him a musical."

We all glance at each other, wondering if we can do this while we're all half cut. With a renewed sense of hope, there's no harm in trying.

CHAPTER FORTY-FIVE
Liam

I didn't realise exactly how much I needed this career break until I decided to take it. I got offered five jobs in the end, but I couldn't see myself taking any of them, so… I didn't, choosing instead to invest time into selling the house and taking a well-deserved break.

"Hey!" Katie calls out to me from somewhere inside as I sit in the back yard with a bottle of bud enjoying the last of the late September sun. She helps herself to a bottle from the fridge and joins me on the new patio I finished this afternoon.

"Help yourself," I say sarcastically.

She's sitting across from me at the small bistro table wearing her 'I'm up to something' face. I know it well; it's gotten us into trouble more times than I can count.

"I see the 'For Sale' sign is up outside, any offers yet?" She takes a swig from her bottle.

"It went up yesterday. I've had a few viewings so far and already have two offers. There are six more viewings booked for next week. Do you fancy staying for a takeaway tonight or do you have plans with Jayne?" Looking at her outfit, I assume she's going out.

"Actually, we have plans tonight," She grins.

"We as in…?"

"You, me and Zach. We're going to The Stack. So, go upstairs, sort out that dead animal growing on your face and find something to wear that isn't covered in paint."

"Katie, I don't want to go out."

"Oh, you do, trust me. Get ready!" She pulls me up by the hand. I stand willingly, there's no way she could lift me, and I know there is no point in arguing with her.

It takes me much longer to get ready than usual, since I haven't so much as trimmed my beard for ages but eventually, I come downstairs wearing a grey polo shirt and jeans and a short beard that makes me look like less of a basket case. I forgot what my jaw line looked like for a while there.

Katie looks me up and down before tousling my hair and giving me a firm nod.

It doesn't take long to get to The Stack where Jayne and Zach are waiting for us. We sit on a long bench table right next to the stage and Zach pushes a cold pint towards me with a gleeful smile.

It feels good to be back with my friends again after spending so much time in solitary, but as the evening progresses there is something obvious missing from our group. I haven't spoken to her since I walked out of her house the morning after her dad's funeral. She told me she needed a clean break and I've tried to respect her wishes, no matter how difficult it is for me.

"How's Harriet?" I ask Jayne a little while later, unable to help myself when we break off into separate conversations.

"Yeah, she's fine." Jayne shrugs before taking a tactical bite of her burger so she can't speak anymore. She looks relieved when we're interrupted by an announcement.

"Good evening, ladies and gents!" A male voice says from the stage. The noisy crowd settles down into a low murmur as they pay attention. "Before our live band starts, we've got something special for you all tonight and to introduce it is none other than Sunderland's very own West End legend, Harriet Adams."

The sound of Harriet's name echoing out around the crowd has my blood racing with adrenaline so quickly my hands are trembling.

I risk a look at our friends and they're very much in on it. What is going on here? Is it some sort of plan to get us in the same room?

Everyone cheers as Harriet strolls onto the stage and stands in front of the mic. She adjusts it to her level and addresses the crowd. She looks as beautiful as ever, her dark wavy hair hanging down her back and her blue-green eyes looking out to the crowd. She looks comfortable, as she always does on stage.

"Thank you for that lovely welcome. I'm Harriet and, as Scott said, I'm a musical theatre performer." She looks around at the crowd before taking a deep, steadying breath and continuing. "A quick bit of back story for you all before I begin. I lost my dad recently and it broke me. Not only that, but I let a rumour ruin my career and I let the one man I've truly loved get away." She pauses as the crowd clap her, urging her on through the difficult topic.

Although my eyes haven't left her, she's yet to look at me. "It's taken a lot of work for me to get to where I am now. Up until last week I was still a mess, but thanks to my friends' encouragement I'm standing here tonight to announce" – she laughs softly as if she can't believe what she's about to say – "That I've decided to write my own musical, based on how I met and fell in love with Liam Wright."

Our eyes finally lock as she says my name and for the first time in god knows how long my chest fills with hope instead of heartache.

"Our story isn't finished yet, obviously, the ending depends on how the next four minutes go." She laughs nervously as the crowd all swing around to look at me, but I pay no attention to them; it might as well be just Harriet and me standing in an empty room. "I really hope we get the chance to fix our happy ever after."

"BRB!" Zach says, clapping me on the back, knocking the air out that I didn't realise I'd been holding.

He and Katie stride towards the stage, leaving me and Jayne in the crowd. Then I notice other familiar faces making their way to the stage too. Oscar, Robert and a small group of others including members of the band and ensemble cast.

Harriet comes back to the tall mic stand with Zach taking a spot next to her at the other.

"This is the title song 'Love in the Wings'," she introduces the song, looking back to me with a smile, and I can't help myself from grinning back up at her.

When Harriet starts singing, there isn't a sound to be heard other than her gorgeous voice. Even the staff pause what they're doing to watch in awe as she recounts our love story from the moment we met and I knocked her off her feet, to the first time fitting her mic and the torture we endured in our efforts to stay away from each other. All the way to the build-up to our first kiss and the sheer bliss of finally being together for that short period of time.

I get a lump in my throat and goosebumps over my body as our relationship and every high and low emotion that comes with it flows out in the lyrics she's written for the world to hear.

The song drifts to a soft close as my heart continues to hammer in my chest. The moment Harriet stops singing, I'm on my feet racing to the front of the stage before even thinking about what I'm going to do. There are only about six steps to get up there and I take them two at a time, hauling myself up onto stage by the handrail so I can get to her as quickly as possible.

I hear a drum roll in the background thanks to the band as anticipation grows, but my focus is on the woman I'm going to spend the rest of my life loving.

When I reach her, her arms fly around my neck and I pull her into me, lifting her off her feet as if the move was choreographed. I kiss her hard, right as the drummer strikes the cymbal and the place erupts with the sounds of cheers and whistling. Hundreds of people are celebrating for us but all I hear is her.

"I love you so much, Liam. I don't want to lose you. I can't lose you," she says through our kisses.

"I'm here, Harriet. I've never wanted to be anywhere else."

Still holding her in my arms, I manage to tear my lips from hers and stroke her hair back from her face so that I can look at her with so much love oozing from every pore. I cup her face in my palm, and her eyes are swimming with happy tears.

"You're writing us a musical!" I laugh. "Babe, that's amazing."

"I didn't know how else to get you back." She laughs lightly as if she can't believe it either and I place her back onto her feet. With one final wave we exit the stage together, hand in hand, passing the host who gives Harriet a hug and claps me on the back in a bro hug.

Instead of heading back to the table with the rest of our friends, I pull Harriet into a secluded spot in the corner so we can talk.

"I've missed you so much." I pull her closer to me again and wrap my arms around her waist, needing to feel her press up against me.

"I'm sorry, Liam." She looks up into my eyes, her soft palm caressing my neck. "I should have been there for you that night after the confrontation with your dad. It was a challenging time for you, and I made things much harder. I'm sorry you had to go through it all alone and I'm sorry I couldn't see past my own issues to see that you needed me."

"Harriet, I'm sorry too. I should have told you from the beginning, if I had then we probably wouldn't be in this situation now."

"Can we focus on putting things right between us?"

"I'd love that, babe. Come here." I cup her face with my hand, pulling her in for a kiss. When she glides her tongue against mine, I have to fight against my urge to pin her up against the nearest wall.

"The sooner we get out there and celebrate with our friends the sooner we can get home and really make up." She raises her eyebrows at me suggestively.

"What are we waiting for?" I pull her by the hand towards the entrance to the courtyard, making her giggle as she jogs to keep up.

"Don't worry, I'm sure we can make it worth the wait." She tugs me back to her side.

"So, what are you planning on doing with our musical?" I hang my arm around her shoulder as we walk through the tables revelling in the fact that we don't need to hide this anymore.

"Well, that's where you come into it," she tells me excitedly. "Are you up for the challenge of producing it with me?" Her eyes are alight with hope and passion.

"Let's do it!" Without a doubt, this is the opportunity I've been waiting for my entire life.

EPILOGUE

Liam

Three Years Later

As the cast return to the stage for their final curtain call, the sold-out crowd in the Sunderland Empire Theatre bursts into a roar of cheers, whistling and clapping.

Katie and Zach stand front and centre as the main characters of our show, a part they've played for almost a year now.

Harriet grins at me from the chorus line. She plays the show version of Katie, Katie plays a version of her and Zach a version of me. When we finalised the script and started to talk about casting, Harriet thought that her playing the main character opposite someone that isn't me was a bit weird, and I totally agree since the story of the musical is our love story.

Harriet reaches out to take my hand and we both walk out to address the crowd. We don't normally do this, but tonight is our 250th show and we have a very important announcement to make.

"Thank you!" I say into the standing mic that waits for us at the edge of the stage and the packed auditorium comes to a silence. "Thank you all so much for coming to our 250th performance!" I pause to allow for the applause and just as well I do because the sound is deafening.

"It really means a lot to us that you came here tonight to watch our story," Harriet says, leaning into me and smiling out to the crowd. "When we wrote this show, I don't think Liam or I expected 'Love in the Wings' to turn into this phenomenon"—I grin at her having finally mastered how to say the word after years of practice—"with such a huge fandom. We've spent years working on this and we really couldn't have done it without the support of our amazing cast and crew. There is a lot that goes on behind the scenes to make a production run and we wouldn't be as successful as we are without them, so can we please give them a huge round of applause!"

Harriet grins at me as she takes in the crowd reaction.

"I also have an announcement," I say, and a shocked Harriet looks at me in curious wonder. I'm not one to step away from our script, but tonight is no normal night and Harriet deserves this experience too. "At the start of the night I asked everyone in our company to stay off the internet because tonight, the nominees for this year's Olivier awards were announced and I didn't want anyone to be disheartened during the show if we didn't get nominated. But now that the show is over, I have some news…"

The excitement on stage is palpable, not to mention the buzz of the audience all waiting with bated breath.

"I'll get to the point." I laugh, looking down at Harriet who is now gripping my bicep, bouncing on the balls of her feet like a mad woman, impatiently waiting for me to speak.

"'Love in the Wings' has received not one, not two, but four nominations for this year's Olivier awards. We have three nominations for individuals: Katie Wright – Best Actress in a musical, Zach Brogan – Best Actor in a musical, Harriet Adams – Best Supporting Actress in a musical. And to top it all off, the show has been nominated for Best Musical!"

This time the cast, crew and crowd erupt into a thunderous celebration from everywhere in the theatre. There's no stopping us and I imagine the sound can be heard from miles away as we leap around on stage celebrating like one big family.

"We did it! Liam! We did it!" Harriet says, battling her way to me again, jumping effortlessly into my arms and wrapping all her limbs tightly around my body. I laugh happily as she plants sloppy kisses all over my face in her excitement before I capture her mouth with mine much to the crowd's approval.

"Your dad would be so proud of you, Harriet," I tell her, looking deep into her blue-green eyes.

"He'd be proud of both of us," she says sincerely, running her fingers through my hair to the nape of my neck and pulling me back to kiss her again.

"Smile, guys." Jayne points her lens at us, capturing this moment for us to treasure for years to come.

"I love you, Harriet." I kiss her again, ignoring the flash from Jayne's camera.

My phone vibrates in my pocket and when I pull it out Di's name appears on the screen. It's been well over three years since I've spoken to Di or my dad, ever since that fateful day in London, but I'm not surprised to see her reaching out now. After all, Harriet and I have achieved the impossible with our little love story. I spent years living under my dad's abusive control, and now he gets to watch me from a distance, living my best life with my best friend and beautiful wife by my side, achieving all the things he always told me I wouldn't.

THE END!

Welcome to Sunderland

This story is set in my home city of Sunderland in the North East of England. Some of the places you read about in this book are real, such as the Sunderland Empire Theatre, Roker Park Bandstand, Roker Pier, Roker and Seaburn Beaches and Hamsterley Forest (granted this is in County Durham, but is always a well-loved day out for many of us here in Sunderland.) We also visit Love Lily and The Stack, two of my favourite places to hang out at when visiting this stretch of coastline.

Although there are many well-known Sunderland locations featured in this book, The Whitton Theatre is entirely fictional and as for the location, I imagine it stands proud on the large grassy area by the white lighthouse at Roker Cliff Park looking out over the North Sea. The design of the theatre itself has been inspired by my favourite venue, the Sunderland Empire where I'm lucky enough to have enjoyed countless shows and performances since I was young.

Sunderland Empire – Inspiration for the Fictional Whitton Empire

The Empire Palace, now known as the Sunderland Empire, was officially opened on the 1st of July 1907 by variety and vaudeville star, Vesta Tilley. It has earned the unofficial nickname The West End of the North East thanks to its size and ability to host large productions typically seen on the London West End such as *Beauty and the Beast*, *Wicked* and the *Lion King,* which returned for a second run in the theatre in March 2023 after a record-breaking tour in 2014.

Just like Liam and Harriet in my story, I was very interested to hear about the ghosts of the Sunderland Empire. Actor and comedian, Sid James suffered a fatal heart attack on stage at the Sunderland Empire in 1976 during a performance of *The Mating Season*. His ghost has been spotted wandering around backstage and in his dressing room. Although Sid is probably the most famous of the Empire's ghosts, the spirits of Vesta Tilley and stage manager Molly Moselle are also said to haunt the front of house. The disappearance of Molly Moselle is still a mystery; she went missing during the show's intermission as she popped out to post a letter never to be seen again.

My top tip: When you visit the Sunderland Empire, really take your time to look up and around, especially when you walk through the main entrance. Can you spot the portraits of famous thespians, a gift from the 2014 Lion King tour, the visible WW2 air raid damage and the original terpsichore that once graced the top of the iconic dome?

(This is not an ad or sponsored piece. This information has been gathered independently by Ellie White and has been fact checked by the Sunderland Empire and was correct at the time of publishing.)

Acknowledgements

To my husband, Adam, and my wonderful babies, Oliver and Hallie, thank you for giving me the love and encouragement I needed to write this book, this one is for you.

A huge thank you to my mam, Dale, and dad, Kevin, for being the best parents anyone could wish for and my brother, my extended family and my besties for always showering me with love.

Dean, Katie, Oscar, Rachael, Robert, Shelley and Steph; I hope you all love the characters named after you. (Sorry, Rach, for making yours a villain.)

This book wouldn't be what it is today without my wonderful editor, Aimee Walker, thank you for your guidance and honesty. I love working with you and long may it continue. Thank you to Enni from Yummy Book Covers for the stunning cover and to my publicist, Claire, from House of Hype for all the support you give me.

Thank you to Katie Brace from Katie Brace Creatives, Steph Durkin from Sunderland Empire and Robert Wilson Baker; for always being on hand to answer my umpteen questions about theatre life! To Emma Millen from BBC Radio Newcastle and BBC upload, thank you for always supporting me and giving me a platform to spread word about my work across the North East and nationally.

I'm so lucky to have met some amazing people on this journey, Melissa, Chels, Lyndsey, Elle, Louise, Margaret and my wonderful street team, I'm so lucky to have found you all.

Finally, to you, my reader. Thank you for reading this story and supporting me on this incredible journey.

About the Author

Ellie White was born and raised in Sunderland and is a proud Mackem!

She lives in Houghton-Le-Spring with her husband and two young children. She supports Sunderland AFC and is a lover of chocolate, rom-coms and musicals.

If you've enjoyed this book please leave a kind review on Amazon, Goodreads or Instagram, not forgetting to tag her! It doesn't have to be much, just a few words will do; it will make all the difference!

Follow her on Instagram @elliewhite_writes or search for her on Facebook, Twitter and Tik Tok to stay up to date with new releases!

Also by Ellie White

<u>Love and London</u>

8 Years ago.

Maggie's life was just as she had planned… Perfect. She had graduated Uni with Honours, had landed her dream job and was married to her childhood sweetheart. One thing that wasn't part of the plan was becoming a widow the night before her 22nd Birthday.

Present time.

Turning 30 has forced Maggie to start asking the difficult questions in life. Should she start using anti-ageing eye cream? How much money should she be paying into her private pension fund each month? Is she finally ready to start dating again?

When Maggie's Dad and his business partner Ray decide to retire early it's up to Maggie and Jake, Ray's arrogant and egotistical son, to take control.

Encouraged by her family and friends, Maggie embarks on an emotional journey of healing and self-discovery as she takes on new challenges, pushes herself from her comfort zone and finds herself on a string of terrible blind dates. All the while Jake tries his best to prove to Maggie that after years of antagonising her, he's not as obnoxious as he has had her believe.

https://mybook.to/B08T4WVT3D

<u>A Wearside Story</u>

A football romance series with a difference.

Book 0.5 Playing For You

A novella included in the Twisted Tropes Anthology - OUT NOW!

Natasha Borthwick is Wearside FC's Number One, but after an embarrassing string of losses, she's not so sure she deserves that title anymore.

Luke Ramshaw is the hottest developer in the gaming industry but as his deadline to complete his funding application fast approaches, he still has no game demo to present.

The pair are thrown together by a meddling mutual connection in a last-ditch attempt to save both Natasha's team and Luke's career. The problem? They didn't exactly get off to a great start, but what happens when they get closer is a whole other ball game.

https://mybook.to/B0BL3WLJ5L

Book 1: Playing For Her

Coming 1st September 2023

A tragic injury forces footballing legend Molly Davison into early retirement. Football is her life and now that she can't play anymore, she embarks on a new path as a coach for Wearside FC.

Captain of the team, Jordan Robinson, is preparing to hang up his boots at the end of the season and after being in the game his entire life, he's having an existential crisis. Not to mention the only woman he's ever had feelings for is back on Wearside, worse still, she's officially off limits.

Molly is Jordan's new coach, and she's building a reputation for herself in the men's game and paving the way for women just like her. Staying away from the team captain should be a no brainer but when their chemistry sizzles on and off the pitch, it's easier said than done.

A romance that was once so easy has new challenges as the pair try to navigate their budding relationship through the world of men's professional football. Will their love risk the reputation Molly has worked so hard to build or can they finally have their happy ever after a second time around?

https://mybook.to/B0BYD85WFH

Printed in Great Britain
by Amazon

24264622R00155